Oliver Optic

Try again

Or, The Trials and Triumphs of Harry West

Oliver Optic

Try again
Or, The Trials and Triumphs of Harry West

ISBN/EAN: 9783337119874

Printed in Europe, USA, Canada, Australia, Japan

Cover: Foto ©Andreas Hilbeck / pixelio.de

More available books at **www.hansebooks.com**

TRY AGAIN

by

OLIVER OPTIC.

BOSTON, LEE & SHEPARD.

TRY AGAIN

OR,

THE TRIALS AND TRIUMPHS

OF

HARRY WEST

A STORY FOR YOUNG FOLKS.

BY

OLIVER OPTIC,

AUTHOR OF "THE BOAT CLUB," "ALL ABOARD," "NOW OR NEVER,"
"TRY AGAIN," "POOR AND PROUD," "IN DOORS
AND OUT," ETC., ETC.

———————

BOSTON:
LEE AND SHEPARD, PUBLISHERS.
NEW YORK:
CHARLES T. DILLINGHAM.

PREFACE.

The story of Harry West is a record of youthful experience, designed to illustrate the necessity and the results of perseverance in well doing. The true success in life is the attainment of a pure and exalted character; and he who, at threescore and ten, has won nothing but wealth and a name, has failed to achieve the noblest purpose of his being. Wealth is success; a true life is a far nobler success. He who has won both has been doubly successful; but he who has become rich by neglecting the mind, the heart, and the soul, has sacrificed the greater good to the less.

The true life is worth all the labor and self-denial it may cost. This is the moral of the story contained in this volume. Harry West's trials are moral trials; his triumphs, moral triumphs. Whatever vicissitudes of fortune may attend him, however exciting the incidents of his career, the real struggle is in the soul, the real victory is the conquest of himself.

He is a pauper boy, having had none of the advantages

1 *   (5)

of parental instruction. If not vicious at the outset, his character is of that kind which as readily lays hold on vice as virtue; it has never been hardened by the hallowed influences of a good home.

Perhaps my older readers may regard his awakening from moral lethargy to moral life and activity as slightly romantic. I wished to exhibit the influence of the pure heart upon those with whom it comes in contact — to show what power even a child may possess to do a great and good work. There are many Little Angels in the world; we have seen and known them. If I have been extravagant, Julia Bryant's example can do no harm.

With many thanks to them for the unexpected favor bestowed on "Bobby Bright," the author presents Harry West to his young friends, trusting that he will prove an acceptable companion, and that, like him, when they fail in any good work, they will "TRY AGAIN."

WILLIAM T. ADAMS.

DORCHESTER, March 26 1857

CONTENTS.

TRY AGAIN.

TRY AGAIN;

OR,

THE TRIALS AND TRIUMPHS OF HARRY WEST.

CHAPTER I.

IN WHICH HARRY WEST AND SQUIRE WALKER DISAGREE ON AN IMPORTANT POINT.

"Boy, come here!"

Squire Walker was a very pompous man; one of the most notable persons in the little town of Redfield, which, the inquiring young reader will need to be informed, as it is not laid down on any map of Massachusetts that I am acquainted with, is situated thirty-one miles south-west of Boston.

I am not aware that Redfield was noted for any thing in particular unless it was noted for Squ e

Walker, as Mount Vernon was noted for Washing·
ton, and Monticello for Jefferson. No doubt the
squire thought he was as great a man as either of
these, and that the world was strangely stupid, be·
cause it did not find out how great a man he really
was. It was his misfortune that he was not born in
the midst of stirring times, when great energy, great
genius, and the most determined patriotism are
understood and appreciated.

Squire Walker, then, was a great man — in his
own estimation. It is true, the rest of the world,
including many of the people of Redfield, had not
found it out; but, as the matter concerned himself
more nearly than any one else, he seemed to be
resigned to the circumstances of his lot. He had
represented the town in the legislature of the state,
was a member of the school committee, one of the
selectmen, and an overseer of the poor. Some men
would have considered all these offices as glory enough
for a lifetime; and I dare say the squire would have
been satisfied, if he had not been ambitious to be·
come one of the county commissioners.

The squire had a very high and proper regard for

his own dignity. It was not only his duty to be a great man, but to impress other people, especially paupers and children, with a just sense of his importance. Consequently, when he visited the poorhouse, he always spoke in the imperative mood. It was not becoming a man of his magnificent pretensions to speak gently and kindly to the unfortunate, the friendless, and the forsaken; and the men and women hated him, and the children feared him, as much as they would have feared a roaring lion.

"Boy, come here!" said Squire Walker, as he raised his arm majestically towards a youth who was picking up "windfalls" under the apple trees in front of the poorhouse.

The boy was dressed in a suit of blue cotton clothes, extensively, but not very skilfully, patched. At least two thirds of the brim of his old straw ha was gone, leaving nothing but a snarly fringe of straws to protect his face from the heat of the sun. But this was the least of the boy's trials. Sun or rain, heat or cold, were all the same to him, if he only got enough to eat, and time enough to sleep.

He straightened his back when Squire Walker

2

spoke to him, and stood gazing with evident astonishment that the distinguished gentleman should
condescend to speak to him.

" Come here, you sir ! Do you hear ? " continued
Squire Walker, upon whom the boy's look of wonder
and perturbation was not wholly lost.

" This way, Harry," added Mr. Nason, the keeper
of the poorhouse, who was doing the honors of the
occasion to the representative of the people of
Kedfield.

Harry West was evidently a modest youth, and
appeared to be averse to pushing himself irreverently
into the presence of a man whom his vivid imagination classed with Alexander the Great and Julius
Cæsar, whose great deeds he had read about in the
spelling book.

Harry slowly sidled along till he came within
about a rod of the great man, where he paused,
apparently too much overawed to proceed any farther.

" Come here, I say," repeated Squire Walker.
" Why don't you take your hat off, and make your
manners ? "

Harry took his hat off, and made his manners, not

very gracefully, it is true; but considering the boy's perturbation, the squire was graciously pleased to let his " manners " pass muster.

" How old are you, boy?" asked the overseer.

" Most twelve," replied Harry, with deference.

" High time you were put to work."

" I do work," answered Harry.

" Not much; you look as fat and lazy as one of my fat hogs."

Mr. Nason ventured to suggest that Harry was a smart, active boy, willing to work, and that he more than paid his keeping by the labor he performed in the field, and the chores he did about the house — an interference which the squire silently rebuked, by turning up his nose at the keeper.

" I do all they want me to do," added the boy, whose tongue seemed to grow wonderfully glib under the gratuitous censure of the notable gentleman.

" Don't be saucy, Master West."

" Bless you, squire! Harry never spoke a saucy word in his life," interposed the friendly keeper.

" He should know his place, and learr how to treat his superiors. You give these boys too much meat, Mr. Nason. They can't bear it. Mush and molasses is the best thing in the world for them."

If any one had looked closely at Harry while the functionary was delivering himself of this speech, he might have seen his eye snap and his chest heave with indignation. He had evidently conquered his timidity, and, maugre his youth, was disposed to stand forth and say, " I too am a man." His head was erect, and he gazed unflinchingly into the eye of the squire.

" Boy," said. the great man, who did not like to have a pauper boy look him in the eye without trembling — " boy, I have got a place for you, and the sooner you are sent to it, the better it will be for you and for the town."

" Where is it, sir ? "

" Where is it ? What is that to you, you young puppy ? " growled the squire, shocked at the boy's presumption in daring to question him.

" If I am going to a place, I would like to know where it is," replied Harry.

" You will go where you are sent ! " roared the squire.

"I suppose I must; but I should like to know where."

"Well, then, you shall know," added the overseer maliciously; for he had good reason to know that the intelligence would give the boy the greatest pain he could possibly inflict. "You are going to Jacob Wire's."

"Where, sir?" asked the keeper, looking at the squire with astonishment and indignation.

"To Jacob Wire's," repeated the overseer.

"Jacob Wire's!" exclaimed Mr. Nason.

"I said so."

"Do you think that will be a good place for the boy?" asked the keeper, trying to smile to cover the indignation that was boiling in his bosom.

"Certainly I do."

"Excuse me, Squire Walker, but I don't."

The overseer stood aghast. Such a reply was little better than rebellion in one of the town's servants, and his blood boiled at such unheard-of plainness of speech to him, late representative to the general court, member of the school committee, one of the selectmen, and an overseer of the poor.

Besides, there was another reason why the temerity of the keeper was peculiarly aggravated. Jacob Wire was the squire's brother-in-law; and though the squire despised him quite as much and as heartily as the rest of the people of Redfield. it was not fitting that any of his connections should be assailed by another. It was not so much the fact, as the source from which it came, that was objectionable.

" How dare you speak to me in that manner, Mr. Nason?" exclaimed the squire. " Do you know who I am?"

Mr. Nason did know who he was, but at that moment, and under those circumstances, he so far forgot himself as to inform the important functionary that he didn't care who he was; Jacob Wire's was not a fit place for a heathen, much less a Christian.

" What do you mean, sir?" gasped the overseer, in his rage.

" I mean just what I say, Squire Walker. Jacob Wire is the meanest man in the county. He half starves his wife and children; and no hired man ever staid there more than a week — he always starved them out in that time."

"If you please, sir, I would rather not go to Mr Wire's," put in Harry, to whom the county jail seemed a more preferable place.

"There, shut up! I say you shall go there!" replied the squire.

"Really, squire, this is too bad. You know Wire as well as any man in town, and —— "

"Not another word, Mr. Nason! Have the boy ready to go to Jacob Wire's to-morrow!" and the overseer, not very well satisfied with the interview hastened away to avoid further argument upon delicate topic.

Harry stood watching the retreating form of the great man of Redfield. The mandate he had spoken was the knell of hope to him. It made the future black and desolate. As he gazed the tears flooded his eyes, and his feelings completely overcame him.

"Don't cry, Harry," said the kind-hearted keeper, taking him by the hand.

"I can't help it," sobbed Harry. "He will whip me, and starve me to death. Don't let him put me 'here."

"I don't know as I can help it, Harry."

" I am willing to work, and work hard to 0 ; but I don't want to be starved to death."

" I will do what I can for you ; but the other overseers do pretty much as Squire Walker tells them to do."

" I *can't* go to Jacob Wire's," burst from Harry's ips, as he seated himself on a rock, and gave way to the violence of his emotions.

" I will see the other overseers ; don't cry, Harry. Hope for the best."

" No use of hoping against such a man as Jacob Wire. If he don't starve me, he will work me to death. I would rather die than go there."

" Well, well ; don't take on so. Perhaps something can be done."

" Something shall be done," added the boy, as he rose from his seat, with an air of determination in keeping with the strong words he uttered.

The keeper's presence was required in the barn, and he left Harry musing and very unhappy about his future prospects. The thought of becoming a member of Jacob Wire's family was not to be enter-tained. The boy was a pauper, and had been trough ap at the expense of the town ; but he seemed to feel that, though fortune and friends had forsaken him, he was still a member of the great human family.

Jacob Wire, with whom it was proposed to apprentice him, had the reputation of being a hard master. He loved money, and did not love any thing else. His heart was barren of affection, as his soul was of good principles ; and though he did not literally starve his family and his help, he fed them upon the poorest and meanest fare that would support human life. The paupers in the poorhouse lived sumptuously, compared with those who gathered around the board of Jacob Wire.

The keeper knew this from experience, for years ago, before he had been appointed to his present situation, he had worked for Wire ; and age and prosperity had not improved him. The more he got, the more he wanted ; the fuller his barn and storehouse, the more stingy he became to those who were desendent upon him.

Harry West was a good boy, and a great favorite with the keeper of the poorhouse. He was always good-natured, willing to work, and never grumbled about his food. He was not only willing to take care of the baby washing days, but seemed to derive pleasure from the occupation. For all these reasons Mr. Nason liked Harry, and had a deep interest in his welfare; something more than a merely selfish interest, for he had suggested to the overseers the propriety of binding him out to learn some good trade.

Harry was sad and disheartened; but he had unlimited confidence in the keeper, and felt sure that he would protect him from such a calamity as being sent to Jacob Wire's. After he had carried the windfalls into the shed, he asked Mr. Nason if he might go down to the river for a little while. The permission given, he jumped over the cow yard wall, and with his eyes fixed in deep thought upon the ground, made his way over the hill to Pine Pleasant, as the beautiful grove by the river's side was called.

The grove extended to the brink of the stream, which in this place widened into a pond. Near the shore was a large flat rock, which was connected with the main land by a log, for the convenience of anglers and bathers. This was a favorite spot with Harry; and upon the rock he seated himself, to sigh over the hard lot which was in store for him. It was not a good way to contend with the trials to which all are subjected; but he had not yet learned that sorrow and adversity are as necessary for man as joy and prosperity. Besides, it was a turning point in his life, and it seemed to him that Jacob Wire's house would be the tomb of all his hopes.

CHAPTER II.

IN WHICH HARRY FINDS A FRIEND, AND A PRAC TICABLE SCHEME FOR RESISTANCE.

My young readers will probably desire to know something about Harry's " antecedents ; " and while the poor fellow is mourning over the hard lot which Squire Walker has marked out for him, we will briefly review his previous history.

Unlike the heroes of modern novels and romances, Harry did not belong to an ancient, or even a very respectable family. We need not trace his genealogy for any considerable period, and I am not sure that tne old records would throw much light on the subject if we should attempt to do so. The accident of birth in our republican land is a matter of very little consequence ; therefore we shall only go back to Harry's father, who was a carpenter by trade, but had a greater passion for New England rum than for chisels and foreplanes.

The bane of New England was the bane of Frank
lin West; for he was a kind-hearted man, a good
husband and a good father, before he was deformed
by the use of liquor. He made good wages, and
supported his little family creditably for several years;
but the vile habit grew upon him to such a degree
that the people of Redfield lost all confidence in him.
As his business decreased, his besetting vice increased
upon him, till he was nothing but the wreck of the
man he had once been. Poverty had come, and want
stared him in the face.

While every body was wondering what would become of Franklin West, he suddenly disappeared,
and no one could form an idea of what had become
of him. People thought it was no great matter.
He was only a nuisance to himself and his family.
Mrs. West was shocked by this sudden and mysterious disappearance. He was her husband, and the
father of her children, and it was not strange that
she wept, and even hoped that he would come back.
The neighbors comforted her, and put her in the way
of supporting herself and the children, so that she
was very soon reconciled to the event.

When West had been gone a month, his wife received a letter from him, informing her that he had determined to stop drinking, and be a man again. He could not keep sober in Redfield, among his old companions, and he was at work in Providence till he could get money enough to pay his expenses to Valparaiso, in South America, where a lucrative place awaited him. He hoped his wife would manage to get along for a few months, when he should be able to send her some money.

Mrs. West was easy again. Her husband was not dead, was not drowned in the river, or lost in the woods ; and her heart was cheered by the prospects of future plenty, which the letter pointed out to her.

A year passed by, and nothing more was heard from Franklin West. The poor, forsaken wife had a hard time to support her little family. The most constant and severe toil enabled her to pinch her way along ; but it was a bitter trial. She had no relations to help her ; and though the neighbors were as kind as neighbors could be, life was a hard struggle.

Then the baby sickened and died. This bereavement seemed to unnerve and discourage her, and though there was one mouth less to feed her strength failed her, and she was unequal to the task. Care and sorrow did their work upon her, and though people said she died of consumption, Heaven knew she died of a broken heart and disappointed hopes.

Harry was four years old when this sad event left him alone in the world. There was none willing to assume the burden of bringing up the lonely little pilgrim, and he was sent to the poorhouse. It was a hard fate for the tender child to be removed from the endearments of a mother's love, and placed in the cheerless asylum which public charity provides for the poor and the friendless.

The child was only four years old; but he missed the fond kiss and the loving caresses of his devoted mother. They were kind to him there, but it was not home, and his heart could not but yearn for those treasures of affection which glittered for him only in the heart of his mother. There was an aching void, and though he could not understand or appreciate his loss, it was none the less painful.

He was a favorite child, not only with the old paupers, but with the keeper and his family; and this circumstance undoubtedly softened the asperities of his lot. As soon as he was old enough, he was required to work as much as the keeper thought his strength would bear. He was very handy about the house and barn, more so than boys usually are; and Mr. Nason declared that, for the three years before it was proposed to send him away, he had more than earned his board and clothes.

He had been at school four winters, and the school-masters were unanimous in their praise. He was a smart scholar, but a little disposed to be roguish.

The moral discipline of the poorhouse was not of the most salutary character. Mr. Nason, though a generous and kind-hearted man, was not as exempla ry in his daily life as might have been desired. Be-sides, one or two of the old paupers were rather cor-rupt in their manners and morals, and were not fit companions for a young immortal, whose mind, like plastic clay, was impressible to the forming power.

The poorhouse was not a good place for the boy, and the wonder is that Harry, at twelve years of age, was not worse than we find him. He had learned to love Mr. Nason, as he had learned to fear and to hate

Squire Walker. The latter seemed to have absolute power at the poorhouse, and to be lord and master in Redfield. But when the overseer proposed to place the boy in the family of a man whom even the paupers looked down upon and despised, his soul rebelled even against the mandate of the powerful magnate of the town.

Harry turned the matter over and over in his mind as he sat upon the rock at Pine Pleasant. At first he tried to reconcile the idea of living with Jacob Wire; but it was a fruitless effort. The poorhouse seemed like a paradise to such a fate.

Then he considered the possibility and the practicability of resisting the commands of Squire Walker. He could not obtain much satisfaction from either view of the difficult problem, and as a happy resort under the trials of the moment, he began to console himself with the reflection that Mr. Nason might prevail with the overseers, and save him from his doom.

He had not much hope from this direction, and while he was turning again to the question of resistance, he heard footsteps in the grove. He did no

3 *

feel like seeing any person and wished he could go out of signt; but there was no retreating without being observed, so he lay down upon the rock to wait till the intruder had passed.

The person approaching did not purpose to let him off so easily; and when Harry heard his step on the log he raised himself up.

"Hallo, Harry! What are you doing here? Taking a nap?"

It was Ben Smart, a boy of fourteen, who lived near the poorhouse. Ben's reputation in Redfield was not A, No. 1; in fact, he had been solemnly and publicly expelled from the district school only three days before by Squire Walker, because the mistress could not manage him. His father was the village blacksmith, and as he had nothing for him to do—not particularly for the boy's benefit—he kept him at school all the year round.

"O, is that you, Ben?" replied Harry, more for the sake of being civil than because he wished to speak to the other.

"What are you doing here?" asked Ben, who evidently did not understand how a boy could be there alone, unless he was occupied about something.

"Nothing."

"Been in the water?"

"No."

"Fishing?"

"No."

Ben was nonplussed. He suspected that Harry had been engaged in some mysterious occupation, which he desired to conceal from him.

"How long you been here?" continued Ben, persistently.

"About half an hour."

Ben stopped to think. He could make nothing of it. It was worse than the double rule of three, which he conscientiously believed had been invented on purpose to bother school boys.

"You are up to some trick, I know. Tell me what you come down here for."

"Didn't come for any thing."

"What is the use of telling that. No feller would come clear down here for nothing."

"I came down to think, then, if you must know,' answered Harry, rather testily

" To think ! Well, that is a good one ! Ain't the poor-farm big enough to do your thinking on ? "

" I chose to come down here."

" Humph ! You've got the blues, Harry. I should think old Walker had been afoul of you, by your looks."

Harry looked up suddenly, and wondered if Ben knew what had happened.

" I should like to have the old rascal down here for half an hour. I should like to souse him into the river, and hold his head under till he begged my pardon," continued Ben

" So should I," added Harry.

" Should you ? You are a good feller, then ! I mean to pay him off for what he did for me the other day. I wouldn't minded being turned out of school. I rather liked the idea ; but the old muttonhead got me up before all the school, and read me such a lecture ! He thinks there isn't any body in the world but him."

" The lecture didn't hurt you," suggested Harry.

" No ; it didn't. But that warn't the worst of 't."

" What else ? "

"My father give me a confounded licking when I got home. I haven't done smarting yet. But I will pay 'em off for it all."

"You mean Squire Walker."

"And the old man, too."

"If I only had a father, I wouldn't mind letting him lick me now and then," replied Harry, to whom home seemed a paradise, though he had never understood it; and a father and mother, though coarse and brutal, his imagination pictured as angels.

"My father would learn you better than that in a few days," said Ben, who did not appreciate his parents, especially when they held the rod.

Harry relapsed into musing again. He thought how happy he should have been in Ben's place. A home, a father, a mother! We value most what we have not; and if the pauper boy could have had t' blessings which crowned his reckless companion's ɩ, it seemed as though he would have been contented and happy. His condescension in regard to the flogging now and then, was a sincere expression of feeling.

"What's old Walker been doing to you, Harry?"

asked Ben, suspecting the cause of the other's gloom.

" He is going to send me to Jacob Wire's to live."

" Whew ! That is a good one ! To die, you mean. Harry, I wouldn't stand that."

" I don't mean to."

" That's right ; I like your spunk. What do you mean to do ? "

Harry was not prepared to answer this question. He possessed a certain degree of prudence, and though it was easy to declare war against so powerful an enemy as Squire Walker, it was not so easy to carry on the war after it was declared. The overseer was a bigger man to him than the ogre in " Puss in Boots." Probably his imagination largely magnified the grandeur of the squire's position, and indefinitely multiplied the resources at his command.

" What do you mean to do ? " repeated Ben, who for some reason or other, took a deep interest in Harry's affairs.

" I don't know. I would rather die than go ; but don't know how I can help myself ' answered the poor boy, gloomily.

"I do."

Harry looked up with interest and surprise. Ben sympathized with him in his trials, and his heart warmed towards him.

"What, Ben?"

"I daresn't tell you now," replied Ben, after a short pause.

"Why not?"

"Can you keep a secret?"

"Of course I can. Did I ever blow on you?"

"No, you never did, Harry. You are a first rate feller, and I like you. But you see, if you should blow on me now, you would spoil my kettle of fish, and your own too."

"But I won't, Ben."

"Promise me solemnly."

"Solemnly," repeated Harry.

"Well, then, I will get you out of the scrape as nice as a cotton nat."

"How?"

"I guess I won't tell you now; but if you will come down here to-night at eleven o'clock, I will let ou into the whole thing."

"Eleven o'clock! I can't come at that time. We all go to bed at eight o'clock."

"Get up and come."

"I can do that; but perhaps Mr Nason will persuade the overseers not to send me to Jacob Wire's."

"I'm glad I didn't tell you, then. But promise me this, Harry: that, whatever happens, you'll hold your tongue."

"I will, Ben."

"And if Nason don't get you off, be here at eleven o'clock. Put on your best clothes, and take every thing you want with you."

"Going to run away?"

"I didn't say so."

Ben made him promise again to be secret, and they separated. Harry had an idea of what his companion intended, and the scheme solved all his doubts. It was a practicable scheme of resistance, and he returned to the poorhouse, no longer fearful of the impending calamity.

CHAPTER III.

IN WHICH HARRY LEAVES THE POORHOUSE, AND TAKES TO THE RIVER.

WHEN Harry reached the poorhouse, Mr. Nason was absent, and one of the paupers told him that he had taken the horse and wagon. He conjectured that the keeper had gone to see the other overseers, to intercede with them in his behalf. He did not feel as much interest in the mission as he had felt two hours before, for Ben Smart had provided a remedy for his grievances, which he had fully decided to adopt.

It was nearly sunset before Mr. Nason returned; and when he came his looks did not seem to indicate a favorable issue. Harry helped him unharness the horse, and as he led him into the barn the keeper opened the subject.

"I have been to see the other overseers, Harry,"

4

ue began, in tones which seemed to promise nothing hopeful.

" I thought likely you had gone."

" As I supposed, they are all afraid of Squire Walker.   They daresn't say their souls are their own."

" Then I must go to Jacob Wire's."

" The other overseers declare, if the squire says so, you must."

" It is a hard case, Mr. Nason," replied Harry, not much disappointed at the result.

" I know it is, Harry.   Perhaps you might try the place, and then, if you found you couldn't stand it we might make another trial to get you off."

" I don't want to go there, any how.   I should like to help duck the squire in the horse pond."

" Well, Harry, I have done all I can for you,' continued Mr. Nason, seating himself on a keg on the barn floor.   " I wish I could help you."

" You have been very good to me, Mr. Nason.   I shall always remember you as the best friend I ever had," replied Harry, the tears streaming down his sun-browned cheeks.

" Never mind that, Harry ; don't cry."

" I can't help it ; you have been so good to me, that I hate to leave you," blubbered Harry.

" I am sorry you must leave us ; we shall miss you about the place, and I wish it was so that you could stay. But what makes it ten times worse, is the idea of your going to Jacob Wire's."

" Mr. Nason," said Harry, dashing down his tears, and looking earnestly at the keeper, " I have made up my mind that I won't go to Wire's any how."

" I don't blame you ; but I don't see how you can fight the squire. He carries too many guns for you, or for me either, for that matter. I have been thinking of something, Harry, though I suppose, if I should speak it out loud, it would be as much as my place here is worth."

" I have been thinking of something, too," continued Harry, with a good deal of emphasis.

" What ? "

" I can't tell even you."

Mr. Nason, sympathizing deeply with his young friend, did not attempt to obtain any knowledge whose possession might be inconvenient to him. He

was disposed to help the boy escape the fate in **store**
for him ; but at the same time, having a family to
support, he did not wish to lose his situation, though,
if the emergency had demanded it, he would probably
have oeen willing to make even this sacrifice.

" I was thinking, Harry, how astonished the squire
would be, when he comes over in the morning to
take you to Jacob Wire's, if he should not happen to
find you here."

" I dare say he would," answered Harry, with a
meaning smile.

" By the way, have you heard from Charles Smith
lately ? You know he went to Boston last spring,
and they say he has got a place, and is doing first
rate there."

The keeper smiled as he spoke, and Harry understood him as well as though he had spoken out th
real thought that was in his mind.

" I suppose others might do as he has done."

" No doubt of it."

Mr. Nason took from his pocket the large shot bag
purse, in which he kept his change, and picked ou
four quarters.

"Here, Harry, take these; when you get over to Wire's, money will keep you from starving. It will almost any where, for that matter."

"How good you are!" exclaimed Harry as he took the four quarters. "You have been a father to me, and one of these days I shall be able to pay you this money back again."

"Don't trouble yourself about that. Keep it; and I wish I had a hundred times as much to give you."

"I shall never forget you, Mr. Nason. I shall be a man one of these days, and we shall meet again."

The supper bell rang, and they separated. Harry felt the spirit of a man stirring within him. He felt that the world had cast him off, and refused him a home, even in the poorhouse. He was determined to push his way through life like a hero, and he nerved himself to meet whatever hardships and trials might be apportioned to him.

After supper he went to his room, gathered up the few articles of clothing which constituted his wardrobe, and tying them up in a bundle, concealed them in a hollow stump back of the barn.

At eight o'clock he went to bed as usual. He felt
no desire to sleep, and would not have dared to do so
if he had. He heard the old kitchen clock strike
ten. The house was still, for all had long ago retired
to their rest, and he could hear the sonorous snores
of the paupers in the adjoining rooms. His heart
beat quick with anxiety. It was a novel position in
which he found himself. He had been accustomed
to do every thing fairly and " above board," and the
thought of rising from his bed and sneaking out of
the house like a thief was repulsive to him. But it
was a good cause, in his estimation, and he did not
waste much sentiment upon the matter. A conspiracy had been formed to cheat him of his hopes and of
his future happiness, and it seemed right to him that
he should flee from those with whom he could not
successfully contend.

Carefully and stealthily he crept out of bed, and
put on his best clothes, which were nothing to boast
of at that, for there was many a darn and many a
patch upon the jacket and the trousers. Stockings
and shoes were luxuries in which Harry was not in-
dulged in the warm season; but he had a pair of
each, which he took under his arm.

Like a mouse he crept down stairs, and reached the back door of the house without having disturbed any of its inmates. There were no locks on the poorhouse doors, for burglars and thieves never invaded the home of the stricken, forsaken paupers.

The door opened with a sharp creak, and Harry was sure he was detected. For several minutes he waited, but no sound was heard, and more carefully he opened the door wide enough to permit his passage out.

He was now in the open air, and a sensation of relief pervaded his mind. He was free. No man was his master in this world, and he had not learned to think much of the other world. As he passed through the cow yard, he heard the old gray mare whinny, and he could not resist the temptation to pay her a parting visit. They had been firm friends for years, and as he entered the barn she seemed to recognize him in the darkness.

"Good by, old Prue. I am going away to leave you,' said Harry, in low tones, as he patted the mare upon her neck. "I hope they will use you well. Next to Mr. Nason, you have been my best friend. Good by, old Prue."

The mare whinnied again, as though she perfectly comprehended this affectionate speech, and wished to express her sympathy with her young friend in her own most eloquent language. Perhaps Harry could not render the speech into the vernacular, but he had a high appreciation of her good feeling, and repeated his caresses.

" Good by, old Prue ; but, before I go, I shall give you one more feed of oats — the very last."

The localities of the barn were as familiar to him as those of his own chamber ; and taking the half peck measure, he filled it heaping full of oats at the grain chest, as readily as though it had been clear daylight.

" Here, Prue, is the last feed I shall give you ; " and he emptied the contents of the measure into the trough. " Good by, old Prue ; I shall never see you again."

The mare plunged her nose deep down into the savory mess, and seemed for a moment to forget her friend in the selfish gratification of her appetite. If she had fully realized the unpleasant fact that Harry was going, perhaps she might have been less selfish ·

for this was not the first time she had been indebted
to him for extra rations.

Passing through the barn, the runaway was again
in the open air. Every thing looked gloomy and sad
to him, and the scene was as solemn as a funeral.
There were no sounds to be heard but the monoto-
nous chirp of the cricket, and the dismal piping of
the frogs in the meadow. Even the owl and the
whip-poor-will had ceased their nocturnal notes, and
the stars looked more gloomy than he had ever seen
them before.

There was no time to moralize over these things,
though, as he walked along, he could not help thinking how strange and solemn every thing seemed on
that eventful night.   It was an epoch in his history ;
one of those turning points in human life, when all
the works of nature and of art, borrowing the spirit
which pervades the soul, assume odd and unfamiliar
forms.   Harry was not old enough or wise enough to
comprehend the importance of the step he was taking ;
still he was deeply impressed by the strangeness within and without.

Taking his bundle from the hollow stump, he

directed his steps owards Pine Pleasant. He walked
very slowly, for his feelings swelled within him,
and retarded his steps. His imagination was busy
with the past, or wandering vaguely to the unex-
plored future, which with bright promises tempted
him to press on to the goal of prosperity. He
yearned to be a man; to leap in an instant over the
years of discipline, that yawned like a great gulf between his youth and his manhood. He wanted to be
a man, that his strong arm might strike great blows;
that he might win his way up to wealth and honor.

Why couldn't he be a great man like Squire
Walker. Squire West wouldn't sound bad.

" One has only to be rich in order to be great,'
thought he. " Why can't I be rich, as well as any
body else? Who was that old fellow that saved up
his fourpe ices till he was worth a hundred thousand
dollars? I can do it as well as he, though I won't
be as mean as they say he was. any how. There are
chances enough to get rich, and if I fail in one thing,
why — I can try again."

Thus Harry mused as he walked along. and fixed a
definite purpose before him to be accomplished in

life. It is true it was not a very lofty or a very noble purpose, merely to be rich ; but he had been obliged to do his own philosophizing. He had not yet discovered the true philosopher's stone. He had concluded, like the alchemists of old, that it was the art of turning any thing into gold. The paupers, in their poverty, had talked most and prayed most for that which they had not. Wealth was to them the loftest ideal of happiness, and Harry had adopted their conclusions. It is not strange, therefore, that Harry's first resolve was to be a rich man.

"Seek ye *first* the kingdom of heaven, and all these things shall be added unto you," was a text which he had often heard repeated; but he did not comprehend its meaning, and he had reversed the proposition, determined to look out for "all these things" first.

The village clock struck eleven, and the peal of the clear notes on the silent air cut short his meditations, and admonished him to quicken his pace, or Ben would reach the place of rendezvous before him. He entered the still shades of Pine Pleasant. but saw nothing of his confederate. Seating himself on the

familiar rock in the river, he returned to his medita
tions.

He had hardly laid down the first proposition in
solving the problem of his future success, before he
was startled by the discovery of a bright light in the
direction of the village. It was plainly a building
on fire, and his first impulse was to rush to the meet·
ing house and give the alarm ; but prudence forbade.
His business was with the great world and the future
not with Redfield and the present.

A few moments later the church bell pealed its
startling notes, and he heard the cry of fire in the
village. The building, whatever it was, had become
a mass of fierce flames, which no human arm could
stay.

While he was watching the exciting spectacle, he
heard footsteps in the grove, and Ben Smart, out of
breath and nearly exhausted, leaped upon the rock.

" So you are here, Harry," gasped he.

" I am, Ben," replied Harry. " Where is the
fire ? "

" We have no time to waste now," panted Ben,
rousing himself anew. " We must be off at once."

Ben descended to the lower side of the rock, and hauled a small flat-bottomed boat out of the bushes that grew on the river's brink.

" Where is the fire, Ben ? " persisted Harry.

" Never mind the fire now ; jump into the boat, and let us be off."

Harry obeyed, and Ben pushed off from the rock.

" Where are you going ? " asked Harry, not much pleased either with the imperative tone or the haughty reserve of his companion.

" Down the river. Take the paddle and steer her ; the current will take her along fast enough. I am so tired I can't do a thing more."

Harry took the paddle and seated himself in the stern of the boat, while Ben, puffing and blowing like a locomotive, placed himself at the bow.

" Tell me now where the fire is," said Harry, whose curiosity would not be longer resisted.

" *Squire Walker's barn.*"

5

CHAPTER IV.

IN WHICH IT IS SHOWN THAT THE NAVIGATION OF THE RIVER IS DIFFICULT AND DANGEROUS.

HARRY was astounded at this information. Ben was exhausted, as though he had been running very hard; besides, he was much agitated — more so than the circumstances of the occasion seemed to justify. In connection with the threat which his companion had uttered that day, these appearances seemed to point to a solution of the burning building. He readily understood that Ben, in revenge for the indignity the squire had cast upon him, had set the barn on fire, and was now running away by the light of it.

This was more than he had bargained for. However il -natured he felt towards the squire for his proposel to send him to Jacob Wire's, it never occurred to him to retaliate by committing a crime. His ideas of Christian charity and of forgiveness were but partially developed; and though he could not feel right towards his powerful enemy, he felt no desire to punish him so severely as Ben had done.

His companion gave him a short answer, and manifested no disposition to enlarge upon the subject; and for several minutes both maintained a profound silence.

The boat, drifting slowly with the current, was passing from the pond into the narrow river, and it required all Harry's skill to keep her from striking the banks on either side. His mind was engrossed with the contemplation of the new and startling event which had so suddenly presented itself to embarrass his future operations. Ben was a criminal in the eye of the law, and would be subjected to a severe penalty if detected.

" I shouldn't have thought you would have done that," Harry observed, when the silence became painful to him.

" Done what ? " asked Ben, sharply.

" Set the barn afire."

" Who said I set it afire ? "

" Well, I can see through a millstone when there is a hole in it."

"I didn't say I set the barn afire."

"I know you didn't; but you said you meant to pay the squire off for what he had done to you."

"I mean to."

"Haven't you done it already?"

"I didn't say I had," answered Ben, who was evidently debating with himself whether he should admit Harry to his confidence.

"But didn't you set the barn afire?"

"What if I did?"

"Why, I should say you run a great risk."

"I don't care for that."

"I see the reason, now, why you wouldn't tell me what you was going to do before."

"We are in for it now, Harry. I meant to pay off the squire, and —— "

"Then you did set the barn afire?"

"I didn't say so; and, more than that, I don't mean to say so. If you can see through a millstone why, just open your eyes — that's all"

"I am sorry you did it, Ben."

"No whining, Harry; be a man."

"I mean to be a man; but I don't think there was any need of burning the barn."

"I do; I couldn't leave Redfield without squaring accounts with Squire Walker."

"Where are you going, Ben?"

"To Boston, of course."

"How shall we get there?"

"We will go by the river, as far as we can; then take to the road."

"But this is George Leman's boat — isn't it?"

"Yes."

"You hooked it?"

"Of course I did; you don't suppose I should mind trifles at such a time as this! But he can have it again, when I have done with it."

"What was the use of taking the boat?"

"In the first place, don't you think it is easier to sail in a boat than to walk? And in the second place, the river runs through the woods for five or six miles below Pine Pleasant; so that no one will be likely to see us. We shall get off without being found out."

"But the river is not deep enough. It is full of rocks about three miles down."

"We won't mind them. We can keep her clear

5 *

of the rocks well enough. When I was down the river last spring, you couldn't see a single rock above water, and we don't draw more than six inches."

" But that was in the spring, when the water was high. I don't believe we can get the boat through."

" Yes, we can ; at any rate, we can jump ashore and tow her down," replied Ben, confidently, though his calculations were somewhat disturbed by Harry's reasoning.

" There is another difficulty, Ben," suggested Harry.

" O, there are a hundred difficulties ; but we mustn't mind them."

" They will miss the boat, and suspect at once who has got it."

" We shall be out of their reach when they miss it.'

" I heard George Leman say he was going a fishing in her to-morrow."

" Did you? Then why didn't you say so before?" retorted Ben, angrily.

" Because you didn't tell me what you were going to do. How could I ? "

" Never mind ; it is no use to cry for spilt milk We will make the best of it."

" We e in for it now."

" That we are ; and if you only stick by me, it
w..l all come out right.   If we get caught, you must
keep a stiff upper lip."

" Never fear me."

" And, above all, don't blow on me."

" Of course I won't."

" Whatever happens, promise that you will stick
by me."

" I will, Ben."

" That's a good fellow, Harry.   On that, we will
take a bit of luncheon, and have a good time of it."

As he spoke, Ben drew out from under the seat in
the bow a box filled with bread and cheese.

" You see we are provisioned for a cruise, Harry,"
added Ben, as he offered the contents of the box to
his companion. " Here is enough to last us two or
hree days."

" But you don't mean to keep on the river so long
as that ? "

" I mean to stick to the boat as long as the navigation will permit," replied Ben, with more energy than
ae had before manifested, for he was recovering from

the perturbation with which the crime he had committed filled his mind.

"There is a factory village, with a dam across the river, six or seven miles below here."

"I know it ; but perhaps we can get the boat round the dam in the night time, and continue ur voyage below. Don't you remember that piece in the Reader about John Ledyard, — how he went down the Connecticut River in a canoe ? "

" Yes ; and you got your idea from that ? "

" I did ; and I mean to have a first rate time of it."

Ben proceeded to describe the anticipated pleasures of the river voyage, as he munched his bread and cheese ; and Harry listened with a great deal of satisfaction. Running away was not such a terrible thing, after all. It was both business and pleasure, and his imagination was much inflated by the brilliant prospect before him. There was something so novel and exciting in the affair, that his first experience was of the most delightful character.

He forgot the crime his companion had committed, and had almost come to regard the burning of the squire's barn as a just and proper retribution upon

him, for conspiring against the rights and privileges
of young America.

My young readers may not know how easy it is
even for a good boy to learn to love the companion-
ship of those who are vicious, and disposed to take
the road which leads down to moral ruin and death.
Those lines of Pope, which are familiar to almost
every school boy, convey a great truth, and a thrilling
warning to those who first find themselves taking
pleasure in the society of wicked men, or wicked
boys : —

> " Vice is a monster of so frightful mien
> As to be hated, needs but to be seen ;
> But seen too oft, familiar with her face,
> We first endure, then pity, then embrace. '

Now, I have not represented my hero, at this stage
of the story, as a very good boy, and it did not require much time to familiarize him with the wickedness which was in Ben's heart, and which he did not
take any pains to conceal. The transition from en-
during to pitying, and from that to embracing, was
sudden and easy, if, indeed, there was any middle
passage between the first and last stage.

I am sorry to say that an hour's fellowship with
Ben, under the exciting circumstances in which we
find them, had led him to think Ben a very good
fellow, notwithstanding the crime he had committed.
I shall do my young reader the justice to believe he
hopes Harry will be a better boy, and obtain higher
and nobler views of duty. It must be remembered
that Harry had never learned to " love God and man "
on the knee of an affectionate mother. He had long
ago forgotten the little prayers she had taught him,
and none were said at the poorhouse. We are sorry
he was no better; but when we consider under what
influences he had been brought up, it is not strange
that he was not a good boy. Above every earthly
good, we may be thankful for the blessing of a good
home, where we have been taught our duty to God,
to our fellow-beings, and to ourselves.

The young navigators talked lightly of the present
and the future, as the boat floated gently along
through the gloomy forest. They heard the Redfield
clock strike twelve, and then one. The excitement
had begun to die out. Harry yawned, for he missed
his accustomed sleep, and felt that a few hours' rest

n his bed at the poorhouse was even preferable to navigating the river at midnight. Ben gaped several times, and the fun was really getting very stale.

Those " who go down to the sea in ships," or navigate the river in boats, must keep their eyes open. It will never do to slumber at the helm ; and Harry soon had a practical demonstration of the truth of the prop- osition. He was so sleepy that he could not possibly keep his eyes open ; and Ben, not having the care of the helm, had actually dropped off, and was bowing as politely as a French dancing master to his compan- ion in the stern. They were a couple of smart sail- ors, and needed a little wholesome discipline to teach them the duty of those who are on the watch.

The needed lesson was soon administered ; for just as Ben was making one of his lowest bows in his semi-conscious condition, the bow of the boat ran upon a concealed rock, which caused her to keel over on one side, and very gently pitch the sleeper into the river.

Of course, this catastrophe brought the com- mander of the expedition to his senses, and roused the helmsman to a sense of his own delinquency ;

though it is clear that, as there were no lighthouses
on the banks of the river, and the intricacies of the
channel had never been defined and charted for the
benefit of the adventurous navigator, no human fore-
thought could have provided against the accident.

Harry put the boat about, and assisted his dripping
shipmate on board again. The ducking he had received did not operate very favorably upon Ben's
temper, and he roundly reproached his companion for
his carelessness. The steersman replied with becoming spirit to this groundless charge, telling him he
had better keep his eyes open the rest of the night.
Wet and chilly as he was, Ben couldn't help growling; and both evidently realized that the affair was
not half as romantic as they had adjudged it to be an
hour or two before.

"Never mind it, Ben. If we fail once let us try
again — that's all."

"Try again? You want to drown me, don't you,"
snarled Ben.

Harry assured him he did not, and called his attention to the sound of dashing waters, which could
now be plainly heard. They were approaching the

rocks, and it was certain from the noise that difficult navigation was before them. Harry proposed to haul up by the river's side, and wait for daylight; to which proposition, Ben, whose ardor was effectually cooled by the bath he had received, readily assented.

Accordingly they made fast the painter to a tree on the shore, and both of them disembarked. While Harry was gathering up a pile of dead leaves for a bed, Ben amused himself by wringing out his wet clothes.

"Suppose we make a fire, Harry?" suggested Ben; and it would certainly have been a great luxury to one in his damp condition.

"No; it will betray us," replied Harry, with alarm.

"Humph! It is easy enough for you to talk, who are warm and dry," growled Ben. "I am going to have a fire, any how."

In vain Harry protested. Ben had some matches in the boat, and in a few minutes a cheerful fire blazed in the forest. As the leader of the enterprise felt its glowing warmth, his temper was sensibly impr 'ed. and he even had the hardihood to laugh a'

his late misfortune. But Harry did not care just
then whether his companion was pleasant or sour,
for he had stretched himself on his bed of leaves, and
was in a fair way to forget the trials and hardships
of the voyage in the deep sleep which makes it " all
night ' with a tired boy.

After Ben was thoroughly dried and warmed. he
placed himself by the side of his fellow-voyager, and
both journeyed together through the quiet shades of
dreamland, leaving no wakeful eye to watch over the
interests of the expedition while they slumbered.

CHAPTER V.

IN WHICH HARRY FIGHTS A HARD BATTLE, AND IS DEFEATED.

THE sun was high in the heavens when the tired boatmen awoke. Unaccustomed as they were to fatigue and late hours, they had been completely overcome by the exertion and exposure of the previous night. Harry was the first to recover his lost senses; and when he opened his eyes, every thing looked odd and strange to him. It was not the rough, but neat and comfortable little room in the poorhouse which greeted his dawning consciousness; it was the old forest and the dashing river. He did not feel quite at home; the affair had been divested of its air of romance, and he felt more like a runaway boy than the hero of a fairy tale.

" Hallo, Ben ! " shouted he, to his sleeping companion.

Ben growled once, and then rolled over, as if angry at being disturbed.

" Ben! We shall be caught, if you don't wake up. There, the clock is striking eight ! " and to give Ben a better idea of where he was, he administered a smart kick in the region of the ribs.

" What are you about ? " snarled Ben, springing to his feet with clinched fists.

" Time we were moving.   Don't you see how high the sun is ?   The clock has just struck eight."

" No matter for that.   We are just as safe here as any where else.   You kick me again, and see where you will be ! "

" Come, come, Ben ; don't get mad."

" Don't kick me, then."

" What are you going to do now ? "

" That's my business.   You do what I tell you, that's all you have to do with it," replied Ben, imperiously, as he walked to the bank of the river to survey the difficulties of the navigation.

" *Is* it ? " asked Harry, not particularly pleased with this interpretation of their relations.

" You better believe it is."

"I don't believe any thing of the kind. I ain't your nigger, any how!" added Harry, with spirit.

"I'll bet you are."

"I'll bet I ain't."

"What are you going to do about it?"

"I'll let you know what I am going to do."

'If you don't mind what I tell you, I'll wallo rou on the spot."

"No, you wont;" and Harry turned on his heel, and leisurely walked off towards the thickest of the forest.

"Where are you going?"

"Off."

"Off where?"

"Do you think I'm going to stay with you, to be treated like a dog!" replied Harry, as he continued his retreat.

Ben started after him, but Harry picked up a stick of wood and stood on the defensive.

"Now, if you don't come back, I'll break your head!" said Ben.

"Look out that your own don't get broke;" and Harry brandished his cudgel in the air.

Ben glanced at the club, and saw from the flash of Harry's bright eye, that he was thoroughly aroused His companion was not to be trifled with, and he was ready to abandon the point.

" Come, Harry, it's no use for us to quarrel," he added, with a forced smile.

" I know that ; but I won't be trod upon by you, any body else."

' I don't want to tread on you."

" Yes, you do ; you needn't think you are going to lord it over me in that way. I will go back to the poorhouse first."

" Let's be friends again, Harry. Throw down your club."   .

" Yes, and let you lick me then! No, you don't! "

" I won't touch you, Harry; upon my word and honor, I won't."

" Humph ! Your word and honor ain't worth much. I'll go back, if you'll behave yourself; but I shall keep the club handy."

" Any way you like ; but let us be off."

Ben changed his tone, and condescended to tell Harry what he meant to do, even at the sacrifice of

his dignity as commander of the expedition. An
appearance at least of good feeling was restored, and
after breakfasting on their bread and cheese, they
embarked again, on what now promised to be a peril-
ous voyage.

For a quarter of a mile below, the bed of the narrow river was spotted with rocks, among which the
water dashed with a fury that threatened the destruction of their frail bark. For a time they seriously
debated the question of abandoning the project, Harry proposing to penetrate the woods in a north-east-
erly direction. Ben, however, could not abandon the
prospect of sailing leisurely down the river when
they had passed the rapids, making the passage without any exertion. He was not pleased with the idea
of trudging along on foot for thirty miles, when the
river would bear them to the city with only a little
difficulty occasionally at the rapids and shoal places.
Perhaps his plan would have been practicable at the
highest stage of water, but the river was now below
its ordinary level.

Ben's love of an easy and romantic time carried
the day, and Harry's practical common sense reason-

ing was of no avail, and a taunt at his cowardice induced him to yield the point.

" Now, Harry, you take one of the paddles, and place yourself in the bow, while I steer," said Ben, as he assumed his position.

" Very well; you shall be captain of the boat, and I will do just as you say ; but I won't be bullied on shore," replied Harry, taking the station assigned him.

" All right; now cast off the painter, and let her slide. Keep both eyes open."

" Never fear me ; I will do my share."

The boat floated out into the current, and was borne rapidly down the swift-flowing stream. They were not very skilful boatmen, and it was more a matter of tact than of strength to keep the boat from dashing on the sharp rocks. For a little way, they did very well, though the passage was sufficiently exciting to call their powers into action, and to suggest a doubt as to the ultimate result of the venture.

They soon reached a place, however, where the river turned a sharp angle, and the waters were furiously precipitated down upon a bed of rocks, which threatened them with instant destruction.

" We shall be smashed to pieces!" exclaimed the foolhardy pilot, as his eye measured the descent of the waters. " Let's try to get ashore."

" Too late now," replied Harry, coolly. " Put her through, hit or miss."

But Ben's courage all oozed out, in the face of this imminent peril, and he made a vain attempt to push the boat towards the shore.

" Paddle your end round, Harry," gasped Ben, in the extremity of fear. " We shall be smashed to pieces."

" Too late, Ben; stand stiff, and make the best of it," answered Harry, as he braced himself to meet the shock.

The rushing waters bore the boat down the stream in spite of the feeble efforts of the pilot to check her progress. Ben seemed to have lost all his self-possession, and stooped down, holding on with both hands at the gunwale.

Down she went into the boiling caldron of waters roaring and foaming like a little Niagara. One hard bump on the sharp rocks, and Harry heard the boards snap under him. He waited for no more, but grasp-

ing the overhanging branches of a willow, which grew
on the bank, and upon which he had before fixed his
eyes as the means of rescuing himself, he sprang up
into the tree, and saw Ben tumbled from the boat
into the seething caldron.

"Save me, Harry!" shouted Ben.

But Harry had to save himself first, which, how·
ever, was not now a difficult matter. Swinging him·
self from branch to branch till he reached the trunk
of the willow, he descended to the ground, without
having even wet the soles of his shoes.

"Save me! save me!" cried Ben, in piteous ac·
cents, as the current bore him down the stream.

"Hold on to the boat," replied Harry, "and I will
be there in a minute."

Seizing a long pole which had some time formed
part of a fence there, he hastened down the bank to
the water's edge. The water was not very deep,
but it ran so rapidly that Ben could neither swim
nor stand upon the bottom; and but for his companion's promptness, he would undoubtedly have been
drowned. Grasping the long pole which Harry ex·
tended to him, he was drawn to the shore, having

received no other injury than a terrible fright and a good ducking.

"Here we are," said Harry, when his companion was safely landed.

"Yes, here we are," growled Ben; "and it is all your fault that we are here."

"It is my fault that *you* are here; for if I had not pulled you out of the river, you would have been drowned," replied Harry, indignantly; and perhaps he felt a little sorry just then that he had rescued his ungrateful commander.

"Yes, and if you had only done as I told you, and pushed for the shore above the fall, all this would not have happened."

"And if you hadn't been a fool, we should not have tried to go through such a hole. There goes your old boat;" and Harry pointed to the wreck, filled with water, floating down the stream.

"Here they are!" shouted a voice, not far from them.

Harry started, and so did Ben.

"We are caught!" exclaimed Ben.

"No yet," replied Harry, with some trepidation,

as he broke off a piece of the pole that lay at his feet, and retreated from the river. "Take a club, for I am not going to be carried back without fighting for it."

A survey of the ground and of the pursuers enabled him to prepare for the future. He discovered at a glance the weakness of the assailants.

"Take a club, Ben. Don't you see there is only one man on this side of the river? and we can easily beat him off."

Ben took the club ; but he seemed not to have the energy to use it. In fact, Harry showed himself better qualified to manage the present interests of the expedition than his companion. . All at once he developed the attributes of a skilful commander, while his confederate seemed to have lost all his cunning and all his determination.

"Now, let us run ; and if we are caught we will fight for it," said Harry.

The boys took to their heels, and having a fair start of their pursuer, they kept clear of him for a considerable distance ; but Ben's wet clothes impeded his progress, and Harry had too much magnanimity to save himself at the sacrifice of his companion.

It was evident, after the chase had continued a short time, that their pursuer was gaining upon them. In vain Harry urged Ben to increase his speed; his progress was very slow, and it was soon apparent to Harry that they were wasting their breath in running when they would need it for the fight.

"Now, Ben, we can easily whip this man, and save ourselves. Be a man, and let us stand by each other to the last."

Ben made no reply; but when Harry stopped, he did the same.

"Keep off! or we will knock your brains out," cried Harry, placing himself in the attitude of defence

But the man took no notice of this piece of brava-do ; and, as he approached, Harry levelled a blow at his head. The man warded it off, and sprang forward to grasp the little rebel.

"Hit him, Ben!" shouted Harry, as he dodged the swoop of his assailant.

To his intense indignation and disgust, Ben, instead of seconding his assault, dropped his club, and fled. He seemed to run a good deal faster than he had run before that day : but Harry did not give up the point.

The man pressed him closely, and he defended him self with a skill and vigor worthy a better cause But it war of no use; or, if it was, it only gave Ben more time to effect his escape.

The unequal contest, however, soon terminated in the capture of our resolute hero, and the man tied his hands behind his back; but he did not dare to leave the young lion to go in pursuit of his less unfortunate, but more guilty, confederate.

" There, Master Harry West, I think you have got into a tight place now," said his captor, whose name was Nathan Leman, brother of the person to whom the boat belonged. " We will soon put you in a place where you won't burn any more barns."

Harry was confounded at this charge, and promptly and indignantly denied it. He had not considered the possibility of being accused of such a crime, and it seemed to put a new aspect upon his case.

" You did not set fire to Squire Walker's barn last night? " replied Leman, incredulously.

" No, I did not."

" Perhaps you can make the squire believe it,' sneered his captor.

" I didn't do it."

" Didn't steal my brother's boat either, did you ? "

" *I* didn't."   .

" Who did ? "

Harry thought a moment. After the mean trick
which Ben Smart had served him, he did not feel
very kindly towards him, but he was not yet prepared
to betray him.

" I didn't," was his reply.

Nathan Leman then conducted his prisoner to the
river's side. By this time the other pursuer, who
had been obliged to ascend the river for a quarter of
a mile before he could cross, joined him.

" Where is the other fellow ? " he asked.

" Couldn't catch him. This one fought like a
young tiger, and I couldn't leave him," replied Nathan. " If you will take Harry up to the village, I
will soon have him."

The other assented, and while Nathan went in
search of Ben, Harry was conducted back to the
village.

The prisoner was sad and depressed in spirits ; but
he did not lose all hope. He was appalled at the

idea of being accused of burning the barn; but Le was innocent, and had a vague assurance that no harm could befall him on that account.

When they entered the village, a crowd gathered around them, eager to learn the particulars of the capture; but without pausing to gratify this curiosity, Harry's conductor led him to the poor house, and placed bim in charge of Mr. Nason.

CHAPTER VI.

IN WHICH HARRY CONCLUDES THAT A DEFEAT IS
SOMETIMES BETTER THAN A VICTORY.

THE keeper of the poorhouse received Harry in sullen silence, and conducted him to the chamber in which he had been ordered to keep him a close prisoner. He had apparently lost all confidence in him, and regretted that he had connived at his escape.

Harry did not like the cold and repulsive deportment of his late friend. Mr. Nason had always been kind to him; now he seemed to have fallen in with Squire Walker's plans, and was willing to be the instrument of the overseer's narrow and cruel policy. Before, he had taken his part against the mighty, so far as it was prudent for him to do so; now, he was willing to go over to the enemy.

This reverse made him sadder than any other cir

7 *

cumstance of his return — sadder than the fear of
punishment, or even of being sent to live with Jacob
Wire.

"I've get back again," said Harry, when they
reached the chamber in which he was to be confined.

"I see you have," replied Mr. Nason, in freezing
tones.

The keeper had never spoken to him in such
tones, and Harry burst into tears. His only friend
had deserted him, and he felt more desolate than
ever before in his life.

"You needn't cry, now," said Mr. Nason, sternly.

"I can't help it," sobbed the little prisoner.

"Can't you?"

Mr. Nason sneered as he spoke, and his sneer
pierced the heart of Harry.

"O Mr. Nason!"

"There — that will do. You needn't blubber any
more. You have made your bed, and now you can
lie in it;" and the keeper turned on his heel to
leave the room.

"Don't leave me yet," pleaded Harry.

"Leave you? What do you want of me? I

suppose you want to tell me I advised you to burn the barn."

" I didn't set the barn afire!" exclaimed Harry, now for the first time realizing the cause of his friend's displeasure.

" Don't lie."

" I speak the truth.   I did not set it afire, or even know that it was going to be set on fire."

Mr. Nason closed the door which he had opened to depart. The firm denial, as well as the tone and manner of the boy, arrested his judgment against him.   He had learned to place implicit confidence in Harry's word; for though he might have told lies to others, he never told them to him.

" Who did burn the barn?" asked the keeper, looking sternly into the eye of the culprit.

Harry hesitated.   A sense of honor and magnanimity pervaded his soul.   He had obtained some false notions; and he did not understand that he could hardly be false to one who had been false to himself — that to help a criminal conceal his crime was to conspire against the peace and happiness of his fellow-beings.   Shabbily as Ben Smart had used

him, he could not at once make up his mind to betray him.

" You don't answer," added Mr. Nason.

" I didn't do it."

" But who did ? "

" I don't like to tell."

" Very well ; you can do as you like.   After what
I had done for you, it was a little strange that you
should do as you have."

" I will tell you all about it, Mr. Nason, if you
will promise not to tell."

" I know all about it.   You and Ben Smart put
your heads together to be revenged on the squire ;
you set his barn afire, and then stole Leman's boat."

" No, sir ; I didn't set the barn afire, nor steal
the boat, nor help to do either."

" You and he were together."

" We were ; and if it wasn't for being mean to
Ben, I would tell you all about it."

" Mean to Ben !   As soon as it was known that
you and Ben were missing, every body in the village
knew who set the barn afire.   All you have got to
do is to clear yourself, if you can ; Ben is condemned
already."

"If you will hear my story I will tell you all about it."

Harry proceeded to narrate every thing that had occurred since he left the house on the preceding night. It was a very clear and plausible statement. He answered all the questions which Mr Nason proposed with promptness, and his replies were consistent.

"I believe you, Harry," said the keeper, when he had finished his examination. "Somehow I couldn't believe you would do such a thing as set the squire's barn afire."

"I wouldn't," replied Harry, warmly, and much pleased to find he had reëstablished the confidence of his friend.

"But it is a bad case. The fact of your being with Ben Smart is almost enough to convict you."

"I shouldn't have been with him, if I had known he set the barn afire."

"I don't know as I can do any thing for you, Harry; but I will try."

"Thank you."

Mr. Nason left him, and Harry had an opportunity

to consider the desperate circumstances of his position. It looked just as though he should be sent
to the house of correction. But he was innocent.
He felt his innocence; as he expressed it to the
keeper afterwards, he "felt it in his bones." It did
not, on further consideration, seem probable that he
would be punished for doing what he had not done,
either as principal or accessory. A vague idea of
an all-pervading justice consoled him; and he soon
reasoned himself into a firm assurance that he should
escape unharmed.

He was in the mood for reasoning just then —
perhaps because he had nothing better to do, or perhaps because the added experience of the last twenty-
four hours enabled him to reason better than before.
His fine scheme of getting to Boston, and there
making a rich and great man of himself, had signally
failed. He did not give it up, however.

"I have failed once, but I will try again," said he
to himself, as the conclusion of the whole matter;
and he picked up an old school book which lay on
the table.

The book contained a story, which he had often

tead, about a man who had met with a long list of misfortunes, as he deemed them when they occurred but which proved to be blessings in disguise.

"Oft from apparent ills our blessings rise.
Act well your part; there all the honor lies."

This couplet from the school books came to his aid, also; and he proceeded to make an application of this wisdom to his own mishaps.

"Suppose I had gone on with Ben. He is a miserable fellow," thought Harry; "he would have led me into all manner of wickedness. I ought not to have gone with him, or had any thing to do with him. He might have made a thief and a robber of me. I know I ain't any better than I should be; but I don't believe I'm as bad as he is. At any rate, I wouldn't set a barn afire. It is all for the best, just as the parson says when any body dies By this scrape I have got clear of Ben, and learned a lesson that I won't forget in a hurry."

Harry was satisfied with this logic, and really believed that something which an older and more devout person would have regarded as a special providence had interposed to save him from a life of infamy and wickedness. It was a blessed experi ence, and his thoughts were very serious and earnest.

In the afternoon, Squire Walker came down to the poorhouse to subject Harry to a preliminary examination. Ben Smart had not been taken, and the pursuers had abandoned the chase.

" Boy," said the squire, when Harry was brought before him ; " look at me."

Harry looked at the overseer with all his might. He had got far enough to despise the haughty little great man. A taste of freedom had enlarged his ideas and developed his native independence, so that he did not quail, as the squire intended he should ; on the contrary, his eyes snapped with the earnestness of his gaze. With an honest and just man, his unflinching eye would have been good evidence in his favor ; but the pompous overseer wished to awe him, rather than get at the simple truth.

" You set my barn on fire," continued the squire.

" I did not," replied Harry, firmly.

" Yes, you did. How dare you deny it ? "

" I did not."

He had often read, and heard read, that passage of Scripture which says, " Let your communications he Yea, yea, Nay, nay; for whatsoever is more than these cometh of evil." Just then he felt the truth of the inspired axiom. It seemed just as though any amount of violent protestations would not help him ; and though the squire repeated the charge half a dozen times, he only replied with his firm and simple denial.

Then Squire Walker called his hired man, upon whose evidence he depended for the conviction of the little incendiary.

" Is that the boy, John ? " asked the squire, pointing to Harry.

" No, sir ; it was a bigger boy than that," replied John, without hesitation.

" Are you sure ? "

" O, very sure."

" It must be that this is the boy," persisted the squire, evidently much disappointed by the testimony of the man.

" I am certain it was a bigger boy than this."

" I feel pretty clear about it, Mr. Nason," added

the squire. " You see, this boy was mad, yesterday, because I wanted to send him to Jacob Wire's. My barn is burned, and it stands to reason he burned it."

" But I saw the boy round the barn night sfore last," interposed John, who was certainly better qualified to be a justice of the peace han his employer.

" I know that; but the barn wasn't burned till last night."

" But Harry couldn't have had any grudge against you night before last," said Mr. Nason.

" I don't know about that," mused the squire, who was apparently trying to reconcile the facts to his theory, rather than the theory to the facts.

John, the hired man, lived about three miles from the squire's house. His father was very sick ; and he had been home every evening for a week, returning between ten and eleven. On the night preceding the fire, he had seen a boy prowling round the barn, who ran away at his approach. The next day, he found a pile of withered grass, dry sticks, and other combustibles heaped against a loose board in the side of the barn. He had informed the squire of the facts, but the worthy justice did not consider them of much moment.

Probably Ben had intended to burn the barn then, but had been prevented from executing his purpose by the approach of the hired man.

"This must be the boy," added the squire.

"He had on a sack coat, and was bigger than this boy," replied John.

"Harry has no sack coat," put in Mr. Nason, eagerly catching at this evidence.

"It is easy to be mistaken in the night. Search him, and see if there are any matches about him."

Undoubtedly this was a very brilliant suggestion of the squire's muddy intellect — as though every man who carried matches was necessarily an incen-diary. But no matches were found upon Harry; and, according to the intelligent justice's perception of the nature of evidence, the suspected party should nave been acquitted.

No matches were found on Harry; but in his acket pocket, carefully enclosed in a piece of brown paper, were found the four quarters of a dollar given to him by Mr. Nason.

"Where did you get those?" asked the squire, sternly.

"They were given to me," replied Harry.

Mr. Nason averted his eyes, and was very uneasy. The fact of having given this money to Harry went to show that he had been privy to his escape; and his kind act seemed to threaten him with ruin.

"Who gave them to you?"

Harry made no reply.

"Answer me," thundered the squire.

"I shall not tell," replied Harry.

"You shall not?"

"No, sir."

The squire was nonplussed. The boy was as firm as a hero; and no threats could induce him to betray his kind friend, whose position he fully comprehended.

"We will see," roared the squire.

Several persons who had been present during the examination, and who were satisfied that Harry was innocent of the crime charged upon him, interfered to save him from the consequences of the squire's wrath.

Mr. Nason, finding that his young friend was likely to suffer for his magnanimity, explained the matter — thus turning the squire's anger 'rom the boy to himself.

" So you helped the boy run away — did you?" said the overseer.

" He did not; he told me that money would keep me from starving."

" Did he?"

Those present understood the allusion, and the squire did not press the matter any further. In the course of the examination, Ben Smart had often been alluded to, and the crime was fastened upon him. Harry told his story, which, confirmed by the evidence of the hired man, was fully credited by all except the squire, who had conceived a violent antipathy to the boy.

The examination was informal ; the squire did not hold it as a justice of the peace, but only as a citizen, or, at most, as an overseer of the poor. However, it proved that, as the burning of the barn had been planned before any difficulty had occurred be-

tween the squire and Harry, he had no motive for
doing the deed.

The squire was not satisfied; but the worst he
could do was to commit Harry to the care of Jacob
Wire, which was immediately done.

"I am sorry for you, Harry," whispered Mr.
Nason.

"Never mind; I shall *try again*," he replied, as
he jumped into the wagon with his persecutor.

CHAPTER VII.

IN WHICH HARRY FINDS HIMSELF IN A TIGHT
PLACE, AND EXECUTES A COUNTER MOVEMENT.

" Jacob, here is the boy," said Squire Walker, as
he stopped his horse in front of an old, decayed
house.

Jacob Wire was at work in his garden, by the side
of the house; and when the squire spoke, he straightened his back, regarding Harry with a look of mingled curiosity and distrust. He evidently did not
like his appearance. He looked as though he would
eat too much; and to a man as mean as Jacob, this
was the sum total of all enormities. Besides, the little
pauper had earned a bad reputation within the preceding twenty-four hours, and his new master glanced
uneasily at his barn, and then at the boy, as though
he deemed it unsafe to have such a desperate character about his premises.

"He is a hard boy, Jacob, and will need a little taming. They fed him too high at the poorhouse," continued the squire.

"That spiles boys," replied Jacob, solemnly.

"So it does."

"So, this is the boy that burnt your barn?"

"Well, I don't know. I rather think it was the Smart boy. Perhaps he knew about it, though;" and the squire proceeded to give his brother-in-law the particulars of the informal examination; for Jacob Wire, who could hardly afford to lie still on Sundays, much less other days, had not been up to the village to hear the news.

"You must be pretty sharp with him," said the overseer, in conclusion. "Keep your eye on him all the time, for we may want him again, as soon as they can catch the other boy."

Jacob promised to do the best he could with Harry who, during the interview, had maintained a sullen silence; and the squire departed, assured that he had done his whole duty to the public and to the little pauper.

"Well, boy, it is about sundown now, and I guess

we will go in and get some supper before we do any more. But let me tell you beforehand, you must walk pretty straight here, or you will fare hard."

Harry vouchsafed no reply to this speech, and followed Jacob into the house. His first meal at his new place confirmed all he had heard about the penuriousness of his master. There was very little to eat on the table, but Mrs. Wire gave him the poorest there was — a hard crust of brown bread, a cold potato, and a dish of warm water with a very little molasses and milk in it, which he was expected to imagine was tea.

Harry felt no disposition to eat. He was too sad and depressed, and probably if the very best had been set before him, he would have been equally indifferent.

He ate very little, and Jacob felt more kindly towards him than before this proof of the smallness of his appetite. He had been compelled to get rid of his last boy, because he was a little ogre, and it seemed as though he would eat him out of house and home.

After supper Harry assisted Jacob about the barn,

and it was nearly eight o'clock before they fin
ished.

"Now, boy, it is about bed time, and I will show
you your rooms, if you like," said Jacob. "Before
you go, let me tell you it won't do any good to try
to run away from here, for I am going to borrow
Lenian's bull-dog."

Harry made no reply to this remark, and followed
his master to the low attic of the house, where he
was pointed to a rickety bedstead, which he was to
occupy.

"There, jump into bed afore I carry the candle
off," continued Jacob.

"I don't care about any light. You needn't
wait," replied Harry, as he slipped off his shoes and
stockings.

"That is right; boys always ought to be learnt to
go to bed in the dark," added Jacob, as he departed.

But Harry was determined not to go to bed in the
dark; so, as soon as he heard Jacob's step on the
floor below, he crept to the stairway, and silently descended. He had made up his mind not to wait for
the bull-dog. Pausing in the entry, he heard Jacob

ted his wife that he was going over to Leman's to
borrow his dog ; he was afraid the boy would get up
in the night and set his barn on fire, or run away.
Jacob then left the house, satisfied, no doubt, that the
bull-dog would be an efficient sentinel while the family were asleep.

After allowing time enough to elapse for Jacob to
reach Leman's house, he softly opened the front door
and went out. It was fortunate for him that Mrs.
Wire was as " deaf as a post," or his suddenly ma-
tured plan to " try again " might have been a failuie.
As it was, his departure was not observed. It was
quite dark, and after he had got a short distance from
the house, he felt a reasonable degree of security.

His first purpose was to get as far away from Redfield as possible, before the daylight should come to
betray him ; and, taking the road, he walked as fast
as his legs would carry him towards Boston. Jacob's
house was on the turnpike, which was the direct roal
to the city, and the distance which the squire had
carried him in his wagon was so much clear gain.

He did not feel very sentimental now. The sky
was overshalowed with clouds, so that he could not

see any stars, and the future did not look half so
bright as his fancy had pictured it on the preceding
night.   But he was free again; and free under more
favorable circumstances than before.   This time he
was himself commander of the expedition, and was to
suffer for no one's bad generalship but his own.   Besides, the experience he had obtained was almost a
guarantee of success.   It had taught him the necessity of care and prudence.

The moral lesson he had learned was of infinitely
more value than even the lesson of policy.   For the
first time in his life he was conscious of a deep and
earnest desire to be a good boy, and to become a true
man.   As he walked along, he thought more of being
a good man than of being a rich man.   It was very
natural for him to do so, under the circumstances, for
he had come very near being punished as an incendiary.   The consequences of doing wrong were just
then strongly impressed upon his mind, and he almost shuddered to think he had consented to remain
with Ben Smart after he knew that he burned the
barn.   Ah, it was an exceedingly fortunate thing for
him that he had got rid of Ben as he did.

For two hours he walked as fast as he could, pausing now and then to listen for the sound of any approaching vehicle. Possibly Jacob might have gone to his room, or attic, to see if he was safe, and his escape had been discovered. He could not be too wary, and every sound that reached his waiting ear caused his heart to jump with anxiety.

He heard a clock strike eleven. It was not the Redfield clock, and it was evident that he was approaching Rockville, a factory village, eight miles from his native place. But his legs were failing him. He was exhausted by the labors and the excitement of the day and night, and his strength would hardly hold out till he should get beyond the village.

Seating himself on a rock by the side of the road, he decided to hold a council of war, to determine what should be done. If he went forward, his strength might fail him at the time when a vigorous effort should be required of him. Somebody's dog might bark, and b'ing the "Philistines upon him." He might meet some late walker, who would detain him. It was hardly safe for him to go through the village by night or day, after the search which had been made for Ben Smart. People would be on the lookout, and it would be no hard matter to mistake him for the other fugitive.

On the other hand, he did not like to pause so near Redfield. He had scarcely entered upon the consideration of this side of the question, before his quick ear detected the sound of rattling wheels in the direction from which he had come. His heart beat violently. It was Squire Walker and Jacob Wire, he was sure, in pursuit of him; but his courage did not fail him.

Leaping over the stone wall by the side of the road, he secured the only retreat which the vicinity afforded, and waited, with his heart in his throat, for the coming of the pursuers, as he had assured himself they were. The present seemed to be his only chance of escape, and if he failed now, he might not soon have another opportunity to " try again."

The vehicle was approaching at a furious pace, and as the noise grew more distinct, his heart leaped the more violently. He thought he recognized the sound of Squire Walker's wagon. There was not much use for his fancy to conjure up strange things, for

the carriage soon reached the place where he was
concealed.   .

"Ur-r—woo!" said a big bull-dog, placing his
ugly nose against the wall, behind which Harry was
lying.

"Whoa!" added a voice, which the trembling
fugitive recognized as that of George Leman.

"The dog has scented him," said another — that
of Jacob Wire.

Harry's heart sunk within him, and he felt as faint
as though every drop of blood had been drawn from
his veins.

"I knew the dog would fetch him," said George
Leman, as he leaped from the wagon, followed by
Jacob Wire.   "At him, Tiger!"

In obedience to this command, Tiger drew back a
few steps, and then leaped upon the top of the wall.
The prospect of being torn in pieces by the bull-dog
was not pleasant to Harry, and with a powerful effort
he summoned his sinking energies for the struggle
before him. Grasping two large stones, he stood
erect as the dog leaped on the wall. Inspired by the
imminence of his peril, he hurled one of the stones

at Tiger, the instant he showed his ugly visage above the fence. The missile took effect upon the animal, and he was evidently much astonished at this unusual mode of warfare. Tiger was vanquished, and fell back from the wall, howling with rage and pain.

"Thunder! He has killed my dog!" exclaimed Leman, as he jumped over the wall.

Harry did not wait any longer, but took to his heels, followed by both his pursuers, though not by the dog, which was *hors de combat.* Our hero was in a "tight place," but with a heroism worthy the days of chivalry, he resolved not to be captured.

He had not run far, however, before he realized that George Leman was more than a match for him, especially in his present worn-out condition. He was almost upon him, when Harry executed a counter movement, which was intended to "outflank" his adversary Dodging round a large rock in the field, he redoubled his efforts, running now towards the road where the horse was standing. Leman was a little confused by this sudden action, and for an instant lost ground.

Harry reached the road and leaped the wall at a

single bound: it was a miracle that, in the darkness he had not dashed his brains out upon the rocks, in the reckless leap. The horse was startled by the noise, and his snort suggested a brilliant idea to Harry.

" Go 'long ! " he shouted ; and the horse started towards Rockville at a round pace.

Harry jumped into the wagon over the hind board, and grasping the reins, put the high-mettled animal to the top of his speed.

" Go 'long ! " hallooed Harry, mad with excite-ment.

The horse manifested no feeling of partiality to-ward either of the parties, and seemed as willing to do his best for Harry as for his master.

" Stop ! Stop ! " shouted George Leman, astound-ed at the new phase which the chase had assumed. " Stop ! and I will let you go."

That was quite reasonable.   It was natural that he should prefer to let the fugitive escape, to the alter-native of losing his horse.   George Leman was noted for three things in Redfield ; his boat, his ugly dog, and his fast horse ; and Harry, after stealing the boat

and killing the dog, was in a fair way to deprive him
of his horse, upon which he set a high value. The
boy seemed like his evil genius, and no doubt he was
angry with himself for letting so mean a man as Jacob
Wire persuade him to hunt down such small game.

Harry did not deem it prudent to stop, and in a
few moments had left his pursuers out of sight.
Then he began to breathe freer. He had played a
desperate game, and won the victory; yet he did not
feel like indulging in a triumph. The battle had
been a bitter necessity, and he even regretted the
fate of poor Tiger, whose ribs he had stove in with
a rock.

He passed through Rockville. All was still, save
the roaring of the waters at the dam, and no one
challenged him.

" I am safe, at any rate," said he to himself, when
he had passed the village. " What will be the next
scrape, I wonder? Confound it! They will have
me up for stealing a horse next. But I didn't steal
him. George Leman is a good fellow, and only for
the fun of the thing, he wouldn't have come out on
such a chase. I wouldn't steal any body's horse.
Whoa ! "

Harry hauled up by the road side, and fastened the horse to the fence.

"There, George, you can have your horse again; but I will just put the blanket over him, for he is all of a reeking sweat. It will just show George, when he comes up, that I don't mean him any harm. I hope his dog wasn't killed."

Taking the blanket which lay in the bottom of the wagon, (for George Leman was very careful of his horse, and though it was October, always covered him when he let him stand out at night,) he spread it over him.

"Now, for Number One again," muttered Harry. "I must take to the woods, though I doubt if George will follow me any farther."

So saying, he got over the fence, and made his way across the fields to the woods, which were but a short distance from the road.

CHAPTER VIII.

IN WHICH HARRY KILLS A BIG SNAKE, AND MAKES A NEW FRIEND.

HARRY was not entirely satisfied with what he had done. He regretted the necessity which had compelled him to take George Leman's horse. It looked too much like stealing; and his awakened moral sense repelled the idea of such a crime. But they could not accuse him of stealing the horse; for his last act would repudiate the idea.

His great resolution to become a good and true man was by no means forgotten. It is true, at the very outset of the new life he had marked out for himself, he had been obliged to behave like a young ruffian, or be restored to his exacting guardians. It was rather a bad beginning; but he had taken what had appeared to him the only course.

Was it right for him to run away? On the solu

tion of this problem depended the moral character of the subsequent acts. If it was right for him to run away, why, of course it was right for him to resist those who attempted to restore him to Jacob Wire.

Harry made up his mind that it was right for him to run away, under the circumstances. His new master had been charged to break him down — even to starve him down. Jacob's reputation as a mean and hard man was well merited; and it was his duty to leave without stopping to say good by.

I do not think that Harry was wholly in the right, though I dare say all my young readers will sympathize with the stout hearted little hero. So far, Jacob Wire had done him no harm. He had suffered no hardship at his hands. All his misery was in the future; and if he had staid, perhaps his master might have done well by him, though it is not probable. Still I think Harry was in some sense justifiable. To remain in such a place was to cramp his soul, as well as pinch his body — to be unhappy, if not positively miserable. He might have tried the place, and when he found it could not be endured, fled from it.

It must be remembered that Harry was a pauper and an orphan. He had not had the benefit of parental instruction. It was not from the home of those whom God had appointed to be his guardians and protectors that he had fled; it was from one who regarded him, not as a rational being, possessed of an immortal soul — one for whose moral, mental, and spiritual welfare he was accountable before God, — that he had run away, but from one who considered him as a mere machine, from which it was his only interest to get as much work at as little cost as possible. He fled from a taskmaster, not from one who was in any just sense a guardian.

Harry did not reason out all this; he only felt it. What was Jacob Wire to him? What was even Squire Walker to him? What did they care about his true welfare? Nothing. Harry so understood it, and acted accordingly.

The future was full of trials and difficulties. But his heart was stout; and the events of the last chapter inspired him with confidence in his own abilities. He entered the dark woods, and paused to rest himself. What should he do next?

While he was discussing this question in his own mind, he heard the sound of voices on the road, which was not more than fifty rods distant. It was George Leman and Jacob Wire. In a few minutes he heard the sound of wagon wheels; and soon had the satisfaction of knowing that his pursuers had abandoned the chase, and were returning home.

The little fugitive was very tired and very sleepy. It was not possible for him to continue his journey, and he looked about him for a place in which to lodge. The night was chilly and damp; and as he sat upon the rock, he shivered with cold. It would be impossible to sleep on the wet ground; and if he could, it might cost him his life. It was a pine forest; and there were no leaves on the ground, so that he could not make such a bed as that in which he had slept the previous night.

He was so cold that he was obliged to move about to get warm. It occurred to him that he might get into some barn in the vicinity, and nestle comfortably in the hay; but the risk of being discovered was. too great, and he directed his steps towards the depths of the forest.

After walking some distance, he came to an open place in the woods. The character of the growth had changed, and the ground was covered with young maples, walnuts, and oaks. The wood had been recently cut off over a large area, but there were no leaves of which he could make a bed.

Fortune favored him, however; for, after advancing half way across the open space, he reached one of those cabins erected for the use of men employed to watch coal pits. It was made of board slabs, and covered over with sods. Near it was the circular space on which the coal pit had burned.

At the time of which I write, charcoal was carried to Boston from many towns within thirty miles of the city. Perhaps my young readers may never have seen a coal pit. The wood is set up on the ends of the sticks, till a circular pile from ten to twenty feet in diameter is formed, and two tiers in height. Its shape is that of a cone, or sugar loaf. It is then covered with turf and soil. Fire is communicated to the wood, so that it shall smoulder, or burn slowly, without blazing. Just enough air is admitted to the pit to keep the fire alive. If the air were freely

adm'tted, the pile would burn to ashes. Sometimes
the outer covering of dirt and sods falls in, as the
wood shrinks, permitting the air to rush in and fan
the fire to a blaze. When this occurs, the aperture
must be closed, or the wood would be consumed;
and it is necessary to watch it day and night. The
cabin had been built for the comfort of the men who
did this duty.

Harry's heart was filled with gratitude when he
discovered the rude nut. If it had been a palace, it
could not have been a more welcome retreat. It
is true the stormy wind had broken down the door,
and the place was no better than a squirrel hole; yet
it suggested a thousand brilliant ideas of comfort,
and luxury even, to our worn-out and hunted fu
gitive.

He entered the cabin. The floor was covered
with straw, which completed his ideal of a luxurious
abode. Raising up the door, which had fallen to the
ground, he placed it before the aperture — thus ex-
cluding the cold air from his chamber.

"I'm a lucky fellow," exclaimed Harry, as he
threw himself on the straw. "This place will be a

palace beside Jacob Wire's house. And I can stay
here a month, if I like."

Nestling closely under the side of the hut, he
pulled the straw over him, and soon began to feel
perfectly at home. Only one consideration troubled
him. The commissary department of the establishment could not be relied on. There were no pork
and potatoes in the house, no well-filled grain chest,
no groceries, not even a rill of pure water at hand.
This was an unpromising state of things; and he
began to see that there would be no fun in living in
the woods, where the butcher and the baker would
not be likely to visit him.

Various means of supplying the deficiency suggested themselves. There were rabbits, partridges,
and quails in the woods; he might set a snare, and
catch some of them. But he had no fire to cook
them; and Dr. Kane had not then demonstrated the
healthy and appetizing qualities of raw meat. The
orchards in the neighborhood were accessible; but
prudence seemed to raise an impassable barrier between him and them.

While he was thus considering these matters, he

dropped asleep, and forgot all about his stomach
He was completely exhausted; and no doubt the
owls and bats were astonished as they listened to
the sonorous sounds that came from the deserted
cabin.

Long and deep was his sleep. The birds sang
their matin songs on the tree tops; but he heard
them not. The sun rose, and penetrated the chinks
of the hut; but the little wanderer still slumbered.
The Rockville clock struck nine; and he heard it
not.

I think it was Harry's grumbling stomach that
finally waked him; and it was no wonder that neglected organ grew impatient under the injury put
upon it, for Harry had eaten little or. nothing since
his dinner at the poorhouse on the preceding day.

Jumping out of the heap of straw in which he had
" cuddled " all night scarcely without moving, he left
the hut to reconnoitre his position. So far as security
was concerned, it seemed to be a perfectly safe place.
He could see nothing of the village of Rockville,
though, beyond the open space, he saw the top of a
chimney; but it was at least half a mile distant.

Just then he did not feel much interested in the scenery and natural advantages of the position. His stomach was imperative, and he was faint from the want of food. There was nothing in the woods to eat. Berry time was past; and the prospect of sup-plying his wants was very discouraging. Leaving the cabin, he walked towards the distant chimney that peered above the tree tops. It belonged to a house that "was set on a hill, and could not be hid."

After going a little way, he came to a cart path, which led towards the house. This he followed, descending a hill into a swamp, which was covered over with alders and birches. At the foot of the declivity he heard the rippling of waters; but the bushes concealed the stream from his view.

He had descended nearly to the foot of the hill when the sound of footsteps reached his ears. His heart beat quick with apprehension, and he paused to listen. The step was soft and light; it was not a man's, and his courage rose. Pat, pat, pat, went the steps on the leafy ground, so gently that his fears were conquered; for the person could be only a child.

Suddenly a piercing shriek saluted his ears
something had occurred to alarm the owner of
the fairy feet which made the soft pat, pat, on the
ground Another shriek, and Harry bounded down
the road like an antelope, heedless of the remon-
strances of his grumbling stomach.

"Mercy! help!" shouted a voice, which Harry
perceived was that of a little girl.

In a moment more, he discovered the young lady
running with all her might towards him.

"Save me!" gasped the girl.

"What is the matter?"

But Harry had scarcely asked the question before
he saw what had alarmed her. Under other circumstances, he would have quailed himself; for, as he
spoke, a great black snake raised his head two or
three feet from the ground directly in front of him.
He was an ugly-looking monster, and evidently intended to attack him. All the chivalry of Harry's
nature was called up to meet the emergency of the
occasion. Seizing a little stick that lay in the path,
he struck sundry vigorous blows at the reptile
which, however, served only to madden, without

disabling, him. Several times he elevated his head
from the ground to strike at his assailant : but the
little knight was an old hand with snakes, and vigorously repelled his assaults. At last, he struck a
blow which laid out his snakeship; and the field was
won, when Harry had smashed his head with a large
rock. The reptile was about four feet and a half
long, and as big round as a small boy's wrist.

"There, miss, he won't hurt you now," said
Harry, panting with his exertions.

"Won't he? Are you sure he is dead?"

"Very sure."

The little girl ventured to approach the dead body
of the snake, and satisfied herself that he could no
harm her.

"What an ugly snake! I was crossing the brook
at the foot of the hill, when he sprang out from
beneath my feet, and chased me. I never was so
frightened in all my life," said the little miss.

"I don't wonder," replied Harry.

"I am very much obliged to you. What is your
name?" asked she, with childish simplicity.

Harry did not like to answer that question, and
made no reply.

" Do you live in Rockville ? " she continued.

" No ; I used to live in Redfield."

" Where do you live now ? "

" I don't live any where."

The little girl wanted to laugh then, it seemed such a funny answer.

" Don't you ?   Who is your father ? "

" I have no father."

" Who is your mother, then ? "

" I have no mother."

" Poor boy !   Then you are an orphan."

" I suppose so.   But, little girl, I don't want you to tell any one that you have seen me. You won't — will you ? "

" Not father and mother ? " asked the maiden, with a stare of astonishment.

" If you please, don't.   I am a poor boy, and have run away from a hard master."

" I won't tell any body."

" And I am very hungry."

" Poor boy !   How lucky that I have lots of goodies in my basket ! " exclaimed she.   " You shall eat all you can."

"1 haven't eat any thing since yesterday noon," replied Harry, as he took a handful of doughnuts she handed him.

" Sit down on this rock, and do eat all you want. I never knew what it was to be very hungry."

Harry seated himself, and proceeded to devour the food the sympathizing little maiden had given him, while she looked on with astonishment and delight as he voraciously consumed cake after cake, without seeming to produce any effect upon the " abhorred vacuum."

CHAPTER IX

IN WHICH HARRY BREAKFASTS ON DOUGHNUTS, AND FINDS THAT ANGELS DO NOT ALWAYS HAVE WINGS.

HARRY was very hungry, and the little girl thought he would never have eaten enough. Since he had told her he had run away, she was deeply interested in him, and had a hundred questions to ask; but she did not wish to bother him while he was eating, he was so deeply absorbed in the occupation.

"What a blessed thing doughnuts are!" laughed she, as Harry levelled on the sixth cake. "I never thought much of them before, but I never shall see a doughnut again without thinking of you."

Our hero was perfectly willing to believe that doughnuts were a very beneficent institution; but just then he was too busily occupied to be sentimental over them.

" What is your name, little girl?" asked Harry
as he crammed half of the cake into his mouth.

" I have a great mind not to tell you, because
you wouldn't tell me what yours is," replied she,
roguishly.

" You see how it is with me. I have run away
from — well, from somewhere."

" And you are afraid I will tell? I won't though.
But, as you killed the snake, I shall tell you. My
name is Julia Bryant."

" Mine is Harry West," replied he, unable to resist
the little lady's argument. " You must not tell any
one about me for three days, for then I shall be out
of the way."

" Where are you going, Harry? "

" To Boston."

" Are you? They say that none but bad boys run
away. I hope you are not a bad boy." And Julia
glanced earnestly at the fugitive.

" I don't think I am."

" I don't think you are, either."

It was a hearty endorsement, and Harry's heart
warmed as she spoke The little maiden was not

more than nine or ten years old, but she seemed to have some skill in reading faces; at least, Harry thought she had. Whatever might be said of himself, he was sure she was a good girl. In short, though Harry had never read a novel in his life, she was a little angel, even if she had no wings. He even went so far as to believe she was a little angel, commissioned by that mysterious something, which wiser and more devout persons would have called a special providence, to relieve his wants with the contents of her basket, and gladden his heart by the sunshine of her sweet smile. There is something in goodness which always finds its way to the face. It makes little girls look prettier than silks, and laces, and ribbons, and embroidery. Julia Bryant was pretty, very pretty. Harry thought so; but very likely it was the doughnuts and her kind words which constituted her beauty.

"I am pretty sure I am not a bad boy," continued Harry; "but I will tell you my story, and you shall judge for yourself."

"You will tell me all of it — won't you?"

"To be sure I will," replied Harry, a little tartly or he misapprehended Julia's meaning.

He thought she was afraid he would not tell his wrong acts; whereas her deep interest in him ren-dered her anxious to have the whole, even to the smallest particulars.

" I shall be so delighted ! I do so love to hear a good story ! " exclaimed Julia.

" You shall have it all; but where were you go-ing ? It will take me a good while."

" I was going to carry these doughnuts to Mrs. Lane. She is a poor widow, who lives over on the back lane. She has five children, and has very hard work to get along. I carry something to her every week."

" Then you are a little angel ! " added Harry, who could understand and appreciate kindness to the poor.

' Not exactly an angel, though Mrs. Lane says I am," replied Julia, with a blush.

" Aunty Gray, over to the poorhouse, used to call every body an angel that brought her any thing good. So I am sure you must be one."

" Never mind what I am now. I am dying to hear your story," interposed Julia, as she seated herself on another rock, near that occupied by Harry.

" Here goes, then ; " and Harry proceeded with his tale, commencing back beyond his remembrance with the traditionary history which had been communicated to him by Mr. Nason and the paupers.

When he came to the period of authentic history or that which was stored up in his memory, he grew eloquent, and the narrative glowed with the living fire of the hero. Julia was quite as much interested as Desdemona in the story of the swarthy Moor. His " round, unvarnished tale," adorned only with the flowers of youthful simplicity, enchained her attention, and she " loved him for the dangers he had passed ; " loved him, not as Desdemona loved, but as a child loves. She was sure now that he was not a bad boy ; that even a good boy might do such a thing as run away from cruel and exacting guardians.

' What a strange story, Harry ! How near you came to being drowned in the river ! I wonder the man had not killed you ! And then they wanted to send you to prison, for setting the barn afire ! " exclaimed Julia, when he had finished the story.

" I came pretty near it ; that's a fact ! " replied

11

Harry, warming under the approbation of his partial auditor.

" And you killed the big dog ? "

" I don't know ; I hope I didn't."

" But you didn't steal the horse ? "

" I didn't mean to steal him."

" No one could call that stealing.   But what are you going to do next, Harry ? "

" I am going to Boston."

" What will you do, when you get there ? "

" I can go to work."

" You are not big enough to work much."

" I can do a good deal."

For some time longer they discussed Harry's story, and Julia regretted the necessity of leaving him to do her errand at Mrs. Lane's.   She promised to see him when she returned, and Harry walked down to the brook to get a drink, while she continued on her way.

Our hero was deeply interested in the little girl l ike the " great guns " in the novels, he was sure she was no ordinary character.   He was fully satisfied in relation to the providential nature of their meeting. She had been sent by that incomprehensible something to furnish him with food, and he trembled when he thought what might have happened if she had not come.

" I can't be a very bad boy," thought he, " or she would not have liked me. Mr. Nason used to say he could tell an ugly horse by the looks of his eye; and the schoolmaster last winter picked out all the bad boys at a glance. I can't be a very bad boy, or she would have found me out. I *know* I am not a bad boy. I feel right, and try to do right."

Harry's imagination invested Julia Bryant with a thousand poetical excellences. That she felt an in-terest in him — one so good as she — was enough to confirm all the noble resolutions he had made, and give him strength to keep them; and as he seated himself by the brook, he thought over his faults, and renewed his determination to uproot them from his character. His meeting with the " little angel," as he chose to regard her, was an oasis in the desert — a place where his moral nature could drink the pure waters of life.

No one had ever before seemed to care much whether he was a good boy or a bad boy. The min-

ıster used now and then to give him a dry lecture;
but he did not seem to feel any real interest in him.
He was a minister, and of course he must preach; not
that he cared whether a pauper boy was a saint or a
sinner, but only to do the work he was hired to do,
and earn his money.

Julia did not preach. Her sweet face was the
" beauty of holiness." She hoped he was not a bad
boy. She liked a good boy; and this was incentive
enough to incur a lifetime of trial and self-sacrifice.
Harry was an orphan. To have one feel an interest
in his moral welfare, to have one wish him to be a
good boy, had not grown stale by long continuance.
He had known no anxious mother, who wished him
to be good, who would weep when he did wrong.
The sympathy of the little angel touched a sensitive
chord in his heart and soul, and he felt that he should
go forward in the great pilgrimage of life with a new
desire to be true to himself, and true to her who had
inspired his reverence

Even a child cannot be good without having it felt
by others. " She hoped he was not a bad boy," were
the words of the little angel; and before she returned

from her errand of mercy, he had repeated them to himself a hundred times. They were a talisman to him, and he was sure he should never be a bad boy in the face of such a wish.

He wandered about the woods for two or three hours, impatient for the return of the little rural goddess who had taken possession of his thoughts, and filled his soul with admiration. She came at last, and glad was the welcome which he gave her.

"I have been thinking of you ever since I left you," said Julia, as she approached the place where he had been waiting her return.

Harry thought this was a remarkable coincidence He had been thinking of her also.

"I hope you didn't think of me as a bad boy," replied he, giving expression to that which was up· permost in his mind.

"I am sure I didn't. I am sure you must be a good boy."

"I am glad you think so; and that will help me be a good boy."

"Will it?"

11 *

" I never had any one to care whether I was good or bad. If you do, you will be the first one."

The little girl looked sad. She had a father and mother who loved her, and prayed for her every day It seemed hard that poor Harry should nave no mother to love him as her mother loved her ; to watch over him day and night, to take care of him when he was sick, and, above all, to teach him to be good. She pitied the lonely orphan, and would gladly have taken him to her happy home, and shared with him all she had, even the love of her mother.

" Poor boy ! " she sighed. " But I have been thinking of something," she added, in more sprightly tones.

" What, Julia ? "

" If you would only let me tell my father that you are here ―― "

" Not for the world ! " cried Harry.

" O, I won't say a word, unless you give me leave ; out my father is rich. ·He owns a great factory and a great farm. He has lots of men to work for him : and my father is a very good man, too. People will do as he wants them to do, and if you will let me tell him your story, he will go over to Redfield and make them let you stay at our house. You shall be my brother then, and we can do lots of things to-gether. Do let me tell him."

"I don't think it would be safe. I know Squire Walker wouldn't let me go to any place where they would use me well."

" What a horrible man he must be ! "

" No ; I think I will go on to Boston."

" You will have a very hard time of it."

"No matter for that."

" They may catch you."

" If they do, I shall try again."

" If they do catch you, will you let my father know it? He will be your friend, for my friends are his friends."

" I will. I should be very glad to have such a friend."

" There is our dinner bell ! " said Julia, as Harry heard the distant sound. " I must go home. How I wish you were going with me ! "

" I wish I was. I may never see you again," add-ed Harry, sadly

" O, you must see me again ! When you get big
you must come to Rockville."

" You will not wish to see the little poorhouse
boy, then."

" Won't I ? I shall always be glad to see the boy
that killed that snake ! But I shall come up after
dinner, and bring you something to eat. Do let me
tell mother you are here."

" I would rather you wouldn't."

" Suppose she asks me what I am going to do with
the dinner I shall bring you ? I can't tell a lie."

" Don't bring any, then. I would rather not have
any dinner than have *you* tell a lie."

Harry would not always have been so nice about
a lie ; but for the little angel to tell a falsehood, why,
it seemed like mud on a white counterpane.

" I won't tell a lie, but you shall have your dinner.
I suppose I must go now."

Harry watched the retreating form of his kind
friend, till she disappeared beyond the curve of the
path, and his blessing went with her.

CHAPTER X.

IN WHICH HARRY FARES SUMPTUOUSLY, AND TAKES LEAVE OF THE LITTLE ANGEL.

WHEN Harry could no longer see the little angel, he fixed his eyes upon the ground, and continued to think of her. It is not every day that a pauper boy sees an angel, or even one whom the enthusiasm of the imagination invests with angelic purity and angelic affections.

In the records of individual experience, as well as in the history of the world, there are certain points of time which are rendered memorable by important events. By referring to a chronological table, the young reader will see the great events which have marked the progress of civilized nations from the lowest depths of barbarism up to their present enlightened state. Every individual, if he had the requisite wisdom, could make up a list of epochs in his own experience. Perhaps he would attach too little importance to some things, too much to others; for we cannot always clearly perceive the influences which assist in forming the character. Some trivial event, far back in the past, which inspired him with a new reverence for truth and goodness, may be forgotten. The memory may not now cherish the look, the smile of approbation, which strengthened the heart, when it was struggling against the foe without or the foe within; but its influence was none the less potent. "It is the last pound which breaks the camel's back;" and that look, that smile, may have closed the door of the heart against a whole legion of evil spirits, and thus turned a life of woe and bitterness into a life of sunshine and happiness.

There are hundreds of epochs in the experience of every person, boy or man — events which raised him up or let him down in the scale of moral existence. Harry West had now reached one of these epochs in his pilgrimage.

To meet a little girl in the woods, to kill a black snake, and thus relieve her from a terrible fright, to say the least, was not a great event, as events are

reckoned in the world; yet it was destined to exert
a powerful influence upon his future career. It was
not the magnitude of the deed performed, or the
chivalrous spirit which called it forth, that made this
a memorable event to Harry; it was the angel visit
— the kindling influence of a pure heart that passed
from her to him. But I suppose the impatient
reader will not thank me for moralizing over two
whole pages, and I leave the further application of
the moral to the discretion of my young friends.

Harry felt strangely — more strangely than he had
ever felt before. As he walked back to the cabin,
every thing seemed to have assumed a new appearance. Somehow the trees did not look as they used
to look. He saw through a different medium. His
being seemed to have undergone a change. He
could not account for it; perhaps he did not try.

He entered the cabin; and, without dropping the
train of thought which Julia's presence suggested, he
busied himself in making the place more comfortable.
He shook up the straw, and made his bed, stuffed
dried grass into the chinks and crannies in the roof,
fastened the door up with some birch withes, and

replaced some of the stones of the chimney which had fallen down. This work occupied him for nearly two hours, though, so busy were his thoughts, they seemed not more than half an hour.

He had scarcely finished making these necessary repairs before he heard the light step of her who fed him, as Elijah was fed by the ravens, for it seemed ake a providential supply. She saw him at the door of the cabin; and she no longer dallied with a walk, but ran with all her might.

"O Harry, I am so glad!" she cried, out of breath, as she handed him a little basket, whose contents were carefully covered with a piece of brown paper.

"Glad of what, Julia?" asked Harry, smiling from sympathy with her.

"I have heard all about it; and I am so glad you are a good boy!" exclaimed she, panting like a pretty fawn which had gambolled its breath away.

"About what?"

"Father has seen and talked with — who was he?"

Harry laughed. How could he tell whom her father had seen and talked with? He was not a magician.

"The man that owned the dog, and the horse, and the boat."

"O! George Leman," replied Harry, now deeply interested in the little maiden's story. "Where did he see him?"

"Over at the store. But I have brought you some dinner; and while you are eating it, I will tell you all about it. Come, there is a nice big rock — that shall be your table."

Julia, full of excitement, seized the basket, and ran to the rock, a little way from the cabin. Pulling off half a dozen great oak leaves from a shrub, she placed them on the rock.

"Here is a piece of meat, Harry, on this plate," she continued, putting it on an oak leaf; "here is a piece of pie; here is some bread and butter; here is cheese; and here is a piece of cold apple pudding. There! I forgot the sauce."

"Never mind the sauce," said Harry; and he could hardly keep from bursting into tears, as he saw how good the little angel was.

It seemed as though she could not have been more an angel, if she had had a pair of wings. The re-

12

diant face was there; the pure and loving heart was there; all was there but the wings, and he could easily imagine them.

And what a dinner! Roast beef, pudding, pie! He was not much accustomed to such luxuries; but just then he did not appreciate the sumptuousness of the feast, for it was eclipsed by the higher consideration of the devotion of the giver.

" Come, eat, Harry! I am so glad!" added Julia.

" So am I. If you feed me as high as this, I shall want to stay here a good while."

" I hope you will."

" Only to-day; to-morrow I must be moving towards Boston."

" I was hoping you would stay here a good long while. I shall be so pleased to bring you your breakfast, and dinner, and supper every day!"

" Your father would not like it."

" I don't know why he shouldn't. You are not very hungry; you don't eat as you did this morning."

" I ate so much then. Tell me, now, what your father said, Julia."

" He saw George Leman; and he told him how you tied his horse to the fence, and how careful you were to put the blanket on him, so that he shouldn't catch cold after his hard run. That was very kind of you, Harry, when you knew they were after you. Father said almost any one would have run the horse till he dropped down. That one thing showed that you were not a bad boy."

" I wouldn't have injured George Leman for any thing," added Harry. " He's a good fellow, and never did me any harm."

" He said, when he found his horse, he was so glad he wouldn't have chased you any farther for all the world. He told father what Mr. Nason said about you — that you were a good boy, had good feelings, and were willing to work. He didn't blame you for not wanting to go to Jacob Wire's — wasn't that the man ? "

" Yes."

" And he didn't blame you for running away. Nobody believes that you set the barn afire; and, Harry, they have caught the other boy — Ben Smart, wasn't it ? "

" Yes, that was his name "

" They caught him in the woods, over the other side of the river."

" Did you find out whether the dog was killed?" asked Harry.

" Mr. Leman said he thought he would get over it; and he has got his boat again."

" I am glad of that; and if any body ever catches me with such a fellow as Ben Smart again, they'll know it."

" You can't think how I wanted to tell father where you were, when he spoke so well of you. He even said he hoped you would get off, and that you must be in the woods around here somewhere. You will let me tell him now — won't you, Harry?"

' I think not."

" Why not, Harry?"

" He may hope I will get off, and still not be will· ing to help me off."

Julia looked very much disappointed; for she had depended upon surprising her father with the story of the snake, and the little fugitive in the woods.

" He will be very good to you," pleaded she.

" I dare say he would; but he may think it his

duty to send me back to Redfield; and Squire Walk‑
er would certainly make me go to Jacob Wire's."

" But you won't go yet."

" To-morrow, Julia."

" I'm afraid you will never get to Boston."

" O, yes, I shall. I don't think it is safe for me
to stay here much longer."

" Why not? Hardly any one ever goes through
the woods here at this time of year but myself."

" Didn't your mother want to know what you
were going to do with the dinner you brought me?"

" No, I went to the store room, and got it. She
didn't see me ; but I don't like to do any thing un‑
known to her."

" You mustn't do it again."

" You must have something to eat."

" You have brought enough to last me while i
stop here. To-morrow morning I must start; so I
suppose I shall not see you again. But I shall never
forget you," said Harry, looking as sad as he felt.

" No, you mustn't go off without any breakfast.
Promise me you will not go till I have brought you
some."

Harry assured Julia he had enough, and ried to persuade her not to bring him any more food; bu. Julia was resolute, and he was obliged to promise Having finished his dinner, she gathered up the remnants of the feast, and put them in the cabin for his supper. She was afraid to remain any longer, lest she might be missed at home; and Harry gallantly escorted her beyond the brook on her return home.

He busied himself during the greater part of the afternoon in gathering dry grass and dead leaves for the improvement of his bed in the cabin. About an hour before sundown, he was surprised to receive another visit from Julia Bryant. She had her little basket in one hand, and in the other she carried a little package.

" I didn't expect to see you again," said Harry, as she approached.

" I don't know as you will like what I have done," she began, timidly; "but I did it for the best."

" I shall like any thing that you have done," an· swered Harry, promptly, " even if you should send me back to Redfield."

" I wouldn't do such a mean thing as that; but I have told somebody that you are here."

" Have you ? " asked Harry, not a little alarmed.

" You will forgive me if I have done wrong — won't you?"

Harry looked at her.   He mistook her anxious appearance for sorrow at what she had done.   He could no' give her pain; so he told her that, whatover she had done, she was forgiven.

" But whom have you told."

" John Lane."

" Who is he?"

" Mrs. Lane's oldest son.   He drives the baggage wagon that goes to Boston every week.   He promted not to lisp a word to a single soul, and that he would be your friend for my sake."

" Why did you tell him?"

" Well, you see, I was afraid you would never get to Boston; and I thought what a nice thing it would be if you could only ride all the way there with John Lane.   John likes me because I carry things to his mother, and I am sure he won't tell."

" How good you are, Julia!" exclaimed Harry. " I may forget every body else in the world; but I shall never forget you."

A tear moistened his eye, as he uttered his enthu-
siastic declaration.

" The worst of it is, John starts at two o'clock —
right in the middle of the night."

" So much the better," replied Harry, wiping away
the tear.

" You will take the wagon on the turnpike, where
the cart path comes out.   But you won't wake up."

" Yes, I shall."

" I am sorry to have you go ; for I like you,
Harry.   You will be a very good boy, when you get
to Boston ; for they say the city is a wicked place."

" I will try."

" There are a great many temptations there, people
say."

" I shall try to be as good as you are," replied
Harry, who could imagine nothing better.   " If I
fail once, I shall try again."

" Here, Harry, I have brought you a good book —
the best of all books.   I have written your name
and mine in it ; and I hope you will keep it and read
it as long as you live.   It is the Bible."

Harry took the package, and thanked her for it.

" I never read the Bible much; but I shall read this for your sake."

" No, Harry; read it for your own sake."

" I will, Julia."

" How I shall long to hear from you! John Lane goes to Boston every week. Won't you write me a few lines, now and then, to let me know how you prosper, and whether you are good or not ? "

" I will. I can't write much; but I suppose I can —— "

" Never mind how you write it, if I can only read it."

The sun had gone down, and the dark shadows of night were gathering over the forest when they parted, but a short distance from Mr. Bryant's house. With the basket which contained provisions for his journey and the Bible in his hand, he returned to the hut, to get what sleep he might before the wagon started.

CHAPTER XI.

IN WHICH HARRY REACHES THE CITY, AND THOUGH OFTEN DISAPPOINTED, TRIES AGAIN.

HARRY entered the cabin, and stretched himself on his bed of straw and leaves ; but the fear that he should not wake in season to take the wagon at the appointed place, would scarcely permit him to close his eyes. He had not yet made up for the sleep he had lost ; and Nature, not sharing his misgiving, at last closed and sealed his eyelids.

It would be presumptuous for me to attempt to inform the reader what Harry dreamed about on that eventful night ; but I can guess that it was about angels, about bright faces and sweet smiles, and that they were very pleasant dreams. At any rate, he slept very soundly, as tired boys are apt to sleep, even when they are anxious about getting up early in the morning.

He woke, at last, with a start; for with his first consciousness came the remembrance of the early appointment. He sprang from his bed, and threw down the door of the cabin. It was still dark; the stars twinkled above, the owls screamed, and the frogs sang merrily around him. He had no means of ascertaining the time of night. It might be twelve; it might be four; and his uncertainty on this point filled him with anxiety. Better too early than too late; and grasping the basket and the Bible, which were to be the companions of his journey, he hastened down the cart path to the turnpike.

There was no sound of approaching wheels to cheer him, and the clock in the meeting house at Rockville obstinately refused to strike. He reached the designated place; there was no wagon there. Perhaps he was too late. The thought filled him with chagrin; and he was reading himself a very severe lesson for having permitted himself to sleep at all, when the church clock graciously condescended to relieve his anxiety by striking the hour.

" One," said he, almost breathless with interest.

" Two," he repeated, loud enough to be heard, if there had been any one to hear him.

"Three;" and he held his breath, waiting for more.

"No more!" he added, with disappointment and chagrin, when it was certain that the clock did not mean to strike another stroke. "I have lost my chance. What a fool I have been! Miss Julia will think that I am a smart fellow, when she finds that her efforts to get me off have been wasted. Why did I go to sleep? I might have known that I should not wake;" and he stamped his foot upon the ground with impatience.

He had been caught napping, and had lost the wagon. He was never so mortified in his life. One who was so careless did not deserve to succeed.

"One thing is clear — it is no use to cry for spilt milk," muttered he, as he jumped over the fence into the road. "I have been stupid, but try again."

Unfortunately, there was no chance to try again. Like thousands of blessed opportunities, it had passed by, never to return. He had come at the eleventh hour, and the door was closed against him. With the wagon it had been "now or never."

Harry got over his impatience, and resolved that

Julia should not come to the cabin, the next morning, to find he had slept when the bridegroom came. He had a pair of legs, and there was the road. It was no use to "wait for the wagon;" legs were made before wagon wheels: and he started on the long and weary pilgrimage.

He had not advanced ten paces before pleasant sounds reached his ears. He stopped short, and listened. A wagon was certainly approaching, and his heart leaped high with hope. Was it possible that John Lane had not yet gone? Retracing his steps, he got over the fence at the place where John was to take him. Perhaps it was not he, after all. He had no right to suppose it was; but he determined to wait till the wagon had passed.

The rumbling noise grew more distinct. It was a heavy wagon, heavily loaded, and approached very slowly; but at last it reached the spot where the impatient boy was waiting.

" Whoa !" said the driver; and the horses stopped.

Harry's heart bounded with joy. Some lucky accident had detained the team, and he had regained his opportunity.

13

" Harry West!" said he on the wagon.

" Joan Lane!" replied Harry, as he leaped ovei the fence.

" You are on hand," added John Lane.

" I am; but I was sure you had gone. It is after three o'clock."

" I know it. I don't generally get off much before this time," answered John. " Climb up here, and let us be moving on."

It was a large wagon, with a sail-cloth cover — one of those regular baggage wagons which railroads have almost driven out of existence in Massachusetts. It was drawn by four horses, harnessed two abreast, and had a high " box " in front for the driver.

Harry nimbly climbed upon the box, and took his seat by the side of John Lane — though that worthy told him he had better crawl under the cover, where he would find plenty of room to finish his nap on a bale of goods.

" I thought likely I should have to go up to the cabin and wake you. Julia told me I must, if you were not on the spot."

' I am glad I have saved you that trouble; but Julia said you would start at two o'clock."

" Well I get off by two or three o'clock. I don't carry the mail, so I ain't so particular. What do you mean to do when you get to Boston ? "

" I mean to go to work."

" What at ? "

" Any thing I can find."

John Lane questioned the little wanderer, and drew from him all the incidents of his past history. He seemed to feel an interest in the fortunes of his companion, and gave him much good advice on practical matters, including an insight into life in the city.

" I suppose Squire Walker would give me fits, if he knew I carried you off. He was over to Rockville yesterday looking for you."

" He won't find me."

" I hope not, my boy; though I don't know as I should have meddled in the matter, if Julia hadn't teased me. I couldn't resist her. She is the best little girl in the world; and you are a lucky fellow to have such a friend."

" I am; she is an angel ; " and when Harry began to think of Julia, he could not think of any thing else, and the conversation was suspended.

It was a long while before either of them spoke
again, and then John advised Harry to crawl into the
wagon, and lie down on the load.   Notwithstanding
his agreeable thoughts, our hero yawned now and
then, and concluded to adopt the suggestion of the
driver.   He found a very comfortable bed on the
bales, softened by heaps of mattings, which were to
be used in packing the miscellaneous articles of the
return freight.

John Lane took things very easily; and as the
horses jogged slowly along, he relieved the monotony
of the journey by singing sundry old-fashioned psalm
tunes, which had not then gone out of use.   He was
a good singer; and Harry was so pleased with the
music, and so unaccustomed to the heavy jolt of the
wagon, that he could not go to sleep at once.

> "While shepherds watched their flocks by night,
>   All seated on the ground,
>   The angel of the Lord came down,
>   And glory shone around."

Again and again John's full and sonorous voice rolled
out these familiar lines, till Harry was fairly lulled
to sleep by the harmonious measures.   The angel of

the Lord had come down for the fortieth time, after the manner of the ancient psalmody, and for the fortieth time Harry had thought of *his* angel, when he dropped off to dream of the "glory that shone around."

Harry slept soundly after he got a little used to the rough motion of the wagon, and it was sunrise before he woke.

"Well, Harry, how do you feel now?" asked John, as he emerged from his lodging apartment.

"Better; I feel as bright as a new pin. Where are we?"

"We have come about twelve miles. Pretty soon we shall stop to bait the team and get some breakfast."

"I have got some breakfast in my basket. Julia gave me enough to last a week. I shan't starve, at any rate."

"No one would ever be hungry in this world, if every body were like Julia. But you shall breakfast with me at the tavern."

"It won't be safe — will it?"

"O, yes; nobody will know you here."

13 *

"Well, I have got some money to pay for any thing I have."

"Keep your money, Harry; you will want it all when you get to Boston."

After going a few miles farther, they stopped at a tavern, where the horses were fed, and Harry ate such a breakfast as pauper never ate before. John would not let him pay for it, declaring that Julia's friends were his friends.

The remaining portion of the journey was effected without any incident worthy of narrating, and they reached the city about noon. Of course the first sight of Boston astonished Harry. His conceptions of a city were entirely at fault; and though it was not a very large city twenty-five years ago, it far exceeded his expectations.

Harry had a mission before him, and he did not permit his curiosity to interfere with that. John drove down town to deliver his load; and Harry went with him, improving every opportunity to obtain work. When the wagon stopped, he went boldly into the stores in the vicinity to inquire if they "wanted to hire a hand."

Now, Harry was not exactly in a condition to pro
duce a very favorable impression upon those to whom
he applied for work. His clothes were never very
genteel, nor very artistically cut and made ; and they
were threadbare, and patched at the knees and el-
bows. A patch is no disgrace to a man or boy, it is
true ; but if a little more care had been taken
adapt the color and kind of fabric in Harry's patches
to the original garment, his general appearance would
undoubtedly have been much improved. Whether
these patches really affected his ultimate success I
cannot say — only that they were an inconvenience
at the outset.

It was late in the afternoon before John Lane had
unloaded his merchandise and picked up his return
freight. Thus far Harry had been unsuccessful ; no
one wanted a boy ; or if they did, they did not want
such a boy as Harry appeared to be. His country
garb, with the five broad patches, seemed to interfere
with the working out of his manifest destiny. Yet
he was not disheartened. Spruce clerks and ill-man-
nered boys laughed at him ; but he did not despond.

"Try again," exclaimed he, as often as he was told
that his services were not required.

When the wagon reached Washington Street, Harry wanted to walk, for the better prosecution of his object; and John gave him directions so that he could find Major Phillips's stable, where he intended to put up for the night.

Harry trotted along among the gay and genteel people that thronged the sidewalk; but he was so earnest about his mission, that he could not stop to look at their fine clothes, nor even at the pictures, the gewgaws, and gimcracks that tempted him from the windows.

"'Boy wanted'" Harry read on a paper in the window of a jeweller's shop. "Now's my time;" and, without pausing to consider the chances that were against him, he entered the store.

"You want a boy — don't you?" asked he of a young man behind the counter.

"We do," replied the person addressed, looking at the applicant with a broad grin on his face.

"I should like to hire out," continued Harry, with an earnestness that would have secured the attention of any man but an idiot.

"Do you? Your name is Joseph — isn't it?"

"No, sir; my name is Harry West."

"O, I thought it was Joseph. The Book says he had a coat of many colors, though I believe it don't say any thing about the trousers," sneered the shop-keeper.

"Never mind the coat or the trousers. If you want to hire a boy, I will do the best I can for you," replied Harry, willing to appreciate the joke of the other, if he could get a place.

"You won't answer for us; you come from the country."

"I did."

"What did you come to Boston for?"

"After work."

"You had better go back, and let yourself to some farmer. You will make a good scarecrow to hang up in the field No crow would ever come near you, I'll warrant."

Harry's blood boiled with indignation at this gratuitous insult. His cheeks reddened, and he looked about him for the means of inflicting summary vengeance upon the poltroon who so wantonly trifled with his glowing aspirations.

"Move on, boy; we don't want you," added the man

"You are a ——"

I will not write what Harry said. It was a vulgar epithet, coupled with a monstrous oath for so small a boy to utter. The shopkeeper sprang out from his counter; but Harry retreated, and escaped him, though not till he had repeated the vulgar and profane expression.

But he was sorry for what he had said before he had gone ten paces.

"What would the little angel say, if she had heard that?" Harry asked himself. "**'Twon't do; I must try again.**"

CHAPTER XII.

IN WHICH HARRY SUDDENLY GETS RICH, AND HAS A CONVERSATION WITH ANOTHER HARRY.

By the time he reached the stable, Harry would have given almost any thing to have recalled the hasty expressions he had used.   He had acquired the low and vulgar habit of using profane language at the poorhouse.   He was conscious that it was not only wicked to do so, but that it was very offensive to many persons who did not make much pretension to piety, or even morality; and, in summing up his faults in the woods, he had included this habit as one of the worst.

She hoped he was a good boy — Julia Bryant, the little angel, hoped so.   Her blood would have frozen in her veins if she had listened to the irreverent words he had uttered in the shop.   He had broken his resolution, broken his promise to the little angel.

on the first day he had been in the city. It was a
bad beginning ; but instead of permitting this first
failure to do right to discourage him, he determined
to persevere — to try again.

A good life, a lofty character, with all the trials
and sacrifices which it demands, is worth working
for ; and those who mean to grow better than they are
will often be obliged to " try again." The spirit may
be willing to do well, but the flesh is weak, and we
are all exposed to temptation. We may make our
good resolutions — and it is very easy to make them ;
but when we fail to keep them — it is sometimes
very hard to keep them — we must not be discouraged, but do as Harry did — TRY AGAIN. The strong
Spirit may conquer the weak Flesh.

" Well, Harry, how did you make out ? " asked
John Lane, when Harry joined him at the stable.

" I didn't make out at all. Nobody seems to want
a boy like me."

" O, well, you will find a place. Don't be discouraged."

" I am not. To-morrow I shall try again."

" I don't know what I shall do with you to-night

Every bed in the tavern up the street, where I stop, is full. I shall sleep with another teamster."

"Never mind me; I can sleep in the wagon. I have slept in worse places than that."

"I will fix a place for you, then."

After they had prepared his bed, Harry drew out his basket, and proceeded to eat his supper. He then took a walk down Washington Street with John, went to an auction, and otherwise amused himself till after nine o'clock, when he returned to the stable.

After John had left him, as he was walking towards the wagon, with the intention of retiring for the night, his foot struck against something which attracted his attention. He kicked it once or twice, to determine what it was, and then picked it up.

"By gracious!" he exclaimed; "it is a pocket book. My fortune is made;" and without stopping to consider the matter any further, he scrambled into the wagon.

His heart jumped with excitement, for his vivid imagination had already led him to the conclusion that it was stuffed full of money. It might contain

14

a hundred dollars, perhaps five hundred; and these sums were about as far as his ideas could reach.

He could buy a suit of new clothes, a new cap, new shoes, and be as spruce as any of the boys he had seen about the city. Then he could go to a boarding house, and live like a prince, till he could get a place that suited him; for Harry, however rich he might be, did not think of living without labor of some kind. He could dress himself up in fine broadcloth, present himself at the jeweller's shop where they wanted a boy, and then see whether he would make a good scarecrow.

Then his thoughts reverted to the cabin, where he had slept two nights, and, of course, to the little angel, who had supplied the commissary department during his sojourn in the woods. He could dress himself up with the money in the pocket book, and, after a while, when he got a place, take the stage for Rockville. Wouldn't she be astonished to see him then, in fine broadcloth! Wouldn't she walk with him over to the spot where he had killed the black snake! Wouldn't she be proud to tell her father that this was the boy she had fed in the woods!

What would she say to him? He had promised to write to her when he got settled, and tell her how he got along, and whether he was good or not. What should he say? How glad she would be to near that he was getting along so finely!

"Stop!" said he to himself. "What have I been thinking about? This pocket book isn't mine."

I am sorry to say it, but Harry really felt sad when the thought occurred to him. He had been building very pretty air castles on this money, and this reflection suddenly tumbled them all down — new clothes, new cap, boarding house, visit to Rockville — all in a heap.

"But I found it," Harry reasoned with himself.

Something within him spoke out, saying, —

"You stole it, Harry."

"No, I didn't; I found it."

"If you don't return it to the owner, you will be a thief," continued the voice within.

"Nobody will know that I found it. I dare say the owner does not want it half so much as I do."

"No matter for that, Harry; if you keep it you will be a thief."

He could not compromise with that voice within. It was the real Harry, within the other Harry, that spoke, and he was a very obstinate fellow, positively refusing to let him keep the pocket book, at any rate.

"What am I about? She hoped I would be a good boy, and the evil one is catching me as fast as he can," resumed Harry.

"Be a good boy," added the other Harry.

"I mean to be, if I can."

"The little angel will be very sad when she finds out that you are a thief."

"I don't mean to be a thief. But this pocket book will make me rich. She never will know any thing about it."

"If she does not, there is One above who will know, and his angels will frown upon you, and stamp your crime upon your face. Then you will go about like Cain, with a mark upon you."

"Pooh!" said the outer Harry, who was sorely tempted by the treasure within his grasp.

"You will not dare to look the little angel in the face, if you steal this money. She will know you.

are not good, then. Honest folks always hold their heads up, and are never ashamed to face any person."

" I won't keep it!" replied the struggling, tempted Flesh. " Why did I think of such a thing?"

He felt strong then, for the Spirit had triumphed over the Flesh. The foe within had been beaten back, at least for the moment; and as he laid his head upon the old coat that was to serve him for a pillow, he thought of Julia Bryant. He thought he saw her sweet face, and there was an angelic smile upon it.

My young readers will remember, after Jesus had been tempted, and said, " Get thee behind me, Satan," that, " behold, angels came and ministered unto him." They came and ministered to Harry after he had cast out the evil thought; they come and minister to all who resist temptation. They come in the heart, and minister with the healing balm of an approving conscience.

Placing the pocket book under his head, with the intention of finding the owner in the morning, he went to sleep. The fatigue and excitement of the

14 *

day softened his pillow, and not once did he open his eyes till the toils of another day had commenced around him. I question whether he would have slept so soundly if he had decided to keep the pocket book.

But the tempter was not banished. He had only been conquered for the moment — subdued only to attack him again. The first thought of the treasure, in the morning, was to covet it. Again he allowed his fancy to picture the comforts and the luxuries which it would purchase.

" No one will know it," he added. " Why shouldn't I keep it ? "

" God will know it ; you will know it yourself," said the other Harry, more faithful and conscientious than the outside Harry, who, it must be confessed, was sometimes disposed to be the " Old Harry."

" No use of being too good. I will keep it."

" *She* hoped you would be a good boy," added the monitor within.

" I will — that is, when I can afford it."

" Be good now, or you never will."

One hundred dollars ! — perhaps five hundred ! It

was a fortune. The temptation was very great. But the little angel — the act would forever banish him from her presence. He would never dare to look at her again, or even to write the letter he had promised.

" Be true to yourself, Harry. Good first, and rich next."

" I will," exclaimed Harry, in an earnest whisper; and again the tempter was cast out.

Once more the fine air castles began to pile themselves up before him, standing on the coveted treasure; but he resolutely pitched them down, and banished them from his mind.

" Where did you lose it?" said a voice near the wagon.

"I don't know. I didn't miss it till this morning; and I have been to every place where I was last night; so I think I must have lost it here, when I put my horse up," replied another.

The first speaker was one of the ostlers; and the moment Harry heard the other voice he started as though a rattlesnake had rattled in his path. Was it possible? As the speaker proceeded, he was satisfied beyond the possibility of a doubt that the voice belonged to Squire Walker.

" Was there much money in it ? " asked the ostler.

" About a hundred and fifty dollars ; and there were notes and other papers of great value," replied Squire Walker.

" Well, I haven't seen or heard any thing about it."

" I remember taking it out of my great-coat pocket, and putting it into a pocket inside of my vest, when I got out of the wagon."

" I don't think you lost it here.   Some of us would have found it, if you had."

Here was a dilemma for Harry.   He had determined to restore the pocket book ; but he could not do so without exposing himself.   Besides, if there had been any temptation to keep the treasure before, it was ten times as great now that he knew it belonged to his enemy.   It would be no sin to keep it from Squire Walker.

" It would be stealing," said the voice within.

" But if I give it to him, he will carry me back to Jacob Wire's.   I'll be — I'll be hanged if I do."

" She hopes you will be a good boy."

There was no resisting this appeal; and again the demon was put down, and the triumph added another laurel to the moral crown of the little hero.

"It will be a dear journey to me," continued Squire Walker. "I was looking all day yesterday after a boy that ran away from the poorhouse, and came to the city for him. I had better let him go."

"Did you find him?"

"No. I brought that money down to put in the bank. It is gone, I suppose. Confound the boy!"

Harry waited no longer; but while his heart beat like the machinery in the great factory at Rockville, he tumbled out of his nest, and slid down the bale of goods to the pavement.

"Ah, Master Harry West! you are here — are you?" exclaimed Squire Walker, springing forward to catch him.

Harry dodged, and kept out of his reach.

"Catch him!" shouted the squire to the ostler.

"Wait a minute, Squire Walker," said Harry. "I won't go back to Jacob Wire's, any how. Just hear what I have got to say; and then, if you want to take me, you may, if you can."

It was evident, even to the squire, that Harry had something of importance to say; and he involuntarily paused to hear it.

"I have found your pocket book, squire, and ——'

"Give it to me, and I won't touch you," cried the overseer, eagerly.

It was clear that the loss of his pocket book had produced a salutary impression on the squire's mind. He loved money, and the punishment was more than he could bear.

"I was walking along here, last night, when I struck my foot against something. I picked it up, and found it was a pocket book. I haven't opened it. Here it is;" and Harry handed him his lost treasure.

"By gracious!" exclaimed he, after he had assured himself that the contents of the pocket book had not been disturbed. "That is more than ever I expected of you, Master Harry West."

"I mean to be honest," replied Harry, proudly.

"Perhaps you do. I told you, Harry, I wouldn't touch you; and I won't," continued the squire. "You may go.'

The overseer was amazed. He had come to Boston with the intention of catching Harry, cost what it might, — he meant to charge the expense to the town; but the recovery of his money had warmed his heart, and banished the malice he cherished towards the boy.

Squire Walker volunteered some excellent advice for the guidance of the little pilgrim, who, he facetiously observed, had now no one to look after his manners and morals — manners first, and morals afterwards. He must be very careful and prudent, and he wished him well. Harry, however, took this wholesome counsel as from whom it came, and was not very deeply impressed by it.

John Lane came to the stable soon after, and congratulated our hero upon the termination of the persecution from Redfield, and, when his horses were hitched on, bade him good by, with many hearty wishes for his future success.

CHAPTER XIII.

IN WHICH HARRY BECOMES A STABLE BOY, AND HEARS BAD NEWS FROM ROCKVILLE.

HARRY was exceedingly rejoiced at the remarkable turn his affairs had taken. It is true, he had lost the treasure upon which his fancy had built so many fine castles; but he did not regret the loss, since it had purchased his exemption from the Redfield persecution. He had conquered his enemy — which was a great victory — by being honest and upright; and he had conquered himself — which was a greater victory — by listening to the voice within him. He had resisted temptation, and the victory made him strong.

Our hero had won a triumph, but the battle field was still spread out before him. There were thousands of enemies lurking in his path, ready to fall apon and despoil him of his priceless treasure — his integrity.

"She hoped he would be a good boy." He had done his duty — he had been true in the face of temptation. He wanted to write to Julia then, and tell her of his triumph — that, when tempted, he had thought of her, and won the victory.

The world was before him; it had no place for idlers, and he must get work. The contents of the basket were not yet exhausted, and he took it to a retired corner to eat his breakfast. While he was thus engaged, Joe Flint, the ostler, happened to see him.

'That is cold comfort," said he. "Why don't you go to the tavern, and have your breakfast like a gentleman?"

"I can't afford it," replied Harry.

"Can't afford it? How much did the man that owned the pocket book give you?"

"Nothing."

"Nothing! I'm blamed if he ain't a mean one!" exclaimed Joe, heartily. "I don't wonder you run away."

"I didn't want any thing. I was too glad to get clear of him to think of any thing else."

"Next time he loses his pocket book, I hope he won't find it."

And with this charitable observation, Joe resumed his labors. Harry finished his meal, washed it down with a draught of cold water at the pump, and was ready for business again. Unfortunately, there was no business ready for him. All day long he wandered about the streets in search of employment; but people did not appreciate his value. No one would hire him or have any thing to do with him. The five patches on his clothes, he soon discovered, rendered it useless for him to apply at the stores. He was not in a condition to be tolerated about one of these: and he turned his attention to the market, the stables, and the teaming establishments, yet with no better success. It was in vain that he tried again; and at night, weary and dispirited, he returned to Major Phillips's stable.

His commissariat was not yet exhausted; and he made a hearty supper from the basket. It became an interesting question for him to consider how he should pass the night. He could not afford to pay ﹀ e of his quarters for a night's lodging at the tavern opposite. There was the stable, however, if he could get permission to sleep there.

"May I sleep in the hay loft, Joe?" he asked, as the ostler passed him.

"Major Phillips don't allow any one to sleep in the hay loft; but perhaps he will let you sleep there. He was asking about you to-day."

"How should he know any thing about me?" said Harry, not a little surprised to find his fame had gone before him.

"He heard about the pocket book, and wanted to see you. He said it was the meanest thing he ever heard of, that the man who lost it didn't give you any thing; and them's my sentiments exactly. Here comes the major; I will speak to him about you."

"Thank you, Joe."

"Major Phillips, this boy wants to know if he may sleep in the hay loft to-night."

"No," replied the stable keeper, short as pie crust.

"This is the boy that found the pocket book, and he hain't got no place to sleep."

"O, is it? Then I will find a place for him to sleep. So, my boy, you are an honest fellow."

" I try to be," replied Harry, modestly.

" If you had kept the pocket book, you might lave lodged at the Tremont House."

" I had rather sleep in your stable, without it."

" Squire Walker was mean not to give you a ten-dollar bill. What are you going to do with yourself?"

" I want to get work; perhaps you have got something for me to do. I am used to horses."

" Well, I don't know as I have."

Major Phillips was a great fat man, rough, vulgar, and profane in his conversation; but he had a kind and sympathizing nature. Though he swore like a pirate sometimes, his heart was in the right place so far as humanity was concerned.

He took Harry into the counting room of the stable, and questioned him in regard to his past history and future prospects. The latter, however, were just now rather clouded. He told the major his experience in trying to get something to do, and was afraid he should not find a place.

The stable keeper was interested in him and in his story. He swore roundly at the meanness of Jacob

Wire and Squire Walker, and commended him for
running away.

"Well, my lad, I don't know as I can do much
for you. I have three ostlers now, which is quite
enough, and all I can afford to pay; but I suppose
I can find enough for a boy to do about the house
and the stable. How much wages do you expect?"

"Whatever you think I can earn."

"You can't earn much for me just now; but if
you are a-mind to try it, I will give you six dollars a
month and your board."

"Thank you, sir; I shall be very glad of the
chance."

"Very well; but if you work for me, you must
get up early in the morning, and be wide awake."

"I will, sir."

"Now we will see about a place for you to
sleep."

Over the counting room was an apartment in which
two of the ostlers slept. There was room for another
bed, and one was immediately set up for Harry's use.

Once more, then, our hero was at home, if a mere
abiding place deserves that hallowed name. It was

15 *

not an elegant, or even a commodious, apartment in which Harry was to sleep. The walls were dingy and black; the beds looked as though they had never been clean; and there was a greasy smell which came from several harnesses that were kept there. It was comfortable, if not poetical; and Harry soon felt perfectly at home.

His first duty was to cultivate the acquaintance of the ostlers. He found them to be rough, good-natured men, not over-scrupulous about their manners or their morals. If it does not occur to my young readers, it will to their parents, that this was not a fit place for a boy — that he was in constant contact with corruption. His companions were good-hearted men; but this circumstance rendered them all the more dangerous. There was no fireside of home, at which the evil effects of communication with men of loose morals would be counteracted. Harry had not been an hour in their society before he caught himself using a big oath — which, when he had gone to bed, he heartily repented, renewing his resolution with the promise to try again.

He was up bright and early the next morning

made a fire in the counting room, and had led out
half the horses in the stable to water, before Major
Phillips came out.   His services were in demand, as
Joe Flint, for some reason, had not come to the stable that morning.

The stable keeper declared that he had gone on
a "spree," and told Harry he might take his
place.

Harry did take his place ; and the ostlers declared
that, in every thing but cleaning the horses, he made
good his place.   The knowledge and skill which he
had obtained at the poorhouse was of great value to
him ; and, at night, though he was very tired, he was
satisfied that he had done a good day's work.

The ostlers took their meals at the house of Major
Phillips, which stood at one side of the stable yard.
Harry did not like Mrs. Phillips very well ; she was
cross, and the men said she was a "regular Tartar."
But he was resolved to keep the peace.   He afterwards found it a difficult matter ; for he had to bring
wood and water, and do other chores about the
house, and he soon ascertained that she was determined not to be pleased with any thing he did.   He

tried to keep his temper, however, and meekly submitted to all her scolding and grumbling.

Thus far, while Harry has been passing through the momentous period of his life with which we commenced his story, we have minutely detailed the incidents of his daily life, so that we have related the events of only a few days. This is no longer necessary. He has got a place, and of course one day is very much like every other. The reader knows him now — knows what kind of boy he is, and what his hopes and expectations are. The reader knows, too, the great moral epoch in his history — the event which roused his consciousness of error, and stimulated him to become better; that he has a talisman in his mind, which can be no better expressed than by those words he so often repeated, " She hoped he would be a good boy." And her angel smile went with him to encourage him in the midst of trial and temptation — to give him the victory over the foes that assailed him.

We shall henceforth give results, instead of a daily record, stopping to detail only the great events of his career.

We shall pass over three months, during which time he worked diligently and faithfully for Major Phillips. Every day had its trials and temptations; not a day passed in which there were none. The habit of using profane language he found it very hard to eradicate; but he persevered; and though he often sinned, he as often repented and tried again, until he had fairly mastered the enemy. It was a great triumph, especially when it is remembered that he was surrounded by those whose every tenth word at least was an oath.

He was tempted to lie, tempted to neglect his work, tempted to steal, tempted in a score of other things. And often he yielded; but the remembrance of the little angel, and the words of the good Book she had given him, cheered and supported him as he struggled on.

Harry's finances were in a tolerably prosperous condition. With his earnings he had bought a suit of clothes, and went to church half a day every Sunday. Besides his wages, he had saved about five dollars from the "perquisites" which he received from customers for holding their horses, running errands, and other little services a boy could perform. He was very careful and prudent with his money; and whenever he added any thing to his little hoard, he thought of the man who had become rich by saving up his fourpences. He still cherished his purpose to become a rich man, and it is very likely he had some brilliant anticipations of success. Not a cent did he spend foolishly, though it was hard work to resist the inclination to buy the fine things that tempted him from the shop windows.

Those who knew him best regarded him as a very strange boy; but that was only because he was a little out of his element. He would have preferred to be among men who did not bluster and swear; but, in spite of them, he had the courage and the fortitude to be true to himself. The little angel still maintained her ascendency in his moral nature.

The ostlers laughed at him when he took out his little Bible, before he went to bed, to drink of the waters of life. They railed at him, called him "Little Pious," and tried to induce him to pitch cents, in the back yard, on Sunday afternoon, instead of going to church. He generally bore these taunts with

patience, though sometimes his high spirit would get
the better of his desire to be what the little angel
wished him to be.

John Lane put up at the stable once a week; and,
every time he returned to Rockville, he carried a
written or a verbal account of the prosperity of the
little pauper boy.   One Sunday, he wrote her a long
letter all about " being good " — how he was tempted, and how he struggled for her sake and for the
sake of the truth.

In return, he often received messages and letters
from her, breathing the same pure spirit which she had
manifested when she " fed him in the wilderness."
These communications strengthened his moral nature,
and enabled him to resist temptation.   He felt just
as though she was an angel sent into the world to
watch over him.   Perhaps he had fallen without
them; at any rate, her influence was very powerful.

About the middle of January, when the earth was
covered with snow, and the bleak, cold winds of
winter blew over the city, John Lane informed Harry
on his arrival, that Julia was very sick with the

scarlet fever and canker rash, and that it was feared she would not recover.

This was the most severe trial of all. He wept when he thought of her sweet face reddened with the flush of fever; and he fled to his chamber, to vent his emotions in silence and solitude.

CHAPTER XIV.

IN WHICH HARRY DOES A GOOD DEED, AND DE-TERMINES TO " FACE THE MUSIC."

WHILE Harry sat by the stove in the ostler's room, grieving at the intelligence he had received from Rockville, a little girl, so lame that she walked with a crutch, hobbled into the apartment.

" Is my father here? " she asked, in tones so sad that Harry could not help knowing she was in distress.

" I don't know as I am acquainted with your father," replied Harry.

" He is one of the ostlers here."

" O, Joseph Flint ! "

" Yes ; he has not been nome to dinner or supper to-day, and mother is very sick."

" I haven't seen him to-day."

16

"O. dear! What will become of us?" sighed the ittle girl, as she hobbled away.

Harry was struck by the sad appearance of the girl, and the desponding words she uttered. Of late, Joe Flint's vile habit of intemperance had grown upon him so rapidly, that he did not work at the stable more than one day in three. For two months, Major Phillips had been threatening to discharge him; and nothing but kindly consideration for his family had prevented him from doing so.

"Have you seen Joe to-day?" asked Harry of one of the ostlers, who came into the room soon after the departure of the little girl.

"No, and don't want to see him," replied Abner, testily; for, in Joe's absence, his work had to be done by the other ostlers, who did not feel very kindly towards him.

"His little girl has just been here after him."

"Very likely he hasn't been home for a week," added Abner. "I should think his family would be very thankful if they never saw him again He is a nuisance to himself and every body else."

"Where does he live?"

"Just up in Avery Street — in a ten-footer there."

"The little girl said her mother was very sick."

"I dare say. She is always sick; and I don't much wonder. Joe Flint is enough to make any one sick. He has been drunk about two thirds of the time for two months."

"I don't see how his family get along."

"Nor I, either."

After Abner had warmed himself, he left the room. Harry was haunted by the sad look and the desponding tones of the poor lame girl. It was a bitter cold evening; and what if Joe's family were suffering with the cold and hunger! It was sad to think of such a thing; and Harry was deeply moved.

"She hoped I would be a good boy. She is very sick now, and perhaps she will die," said Harry to himself. "What would she do, if she were here now?"

He knew very well what she would do, and he determined to do it himself. His heart was so deeply moved by the picture of sorrow and suffering with which his imagination had invested the home of the intemperate ostler, that it required no argument to induce him to go.

But he must go prepared to do something. How‑
ever sweet and consoling may be the sympathy of
others to those in distress, it will not warm the
chilled limbs or feed the hungry mouths; and Harry
thanked God then that he had not spent his money
foolishly upon gewgaws and gimcracks, or in gratify‑
ing a selfish appetite.

After assuring himself that no one was approach‑
ing, he jumped on his bedstead, and reaching p into
a hole in the board ceiling of the room, he took out
a large wooden pill box, which was nearly filled with
various silver coins, from a five-cent piece to a half
dollar.   Putting the box into his pocket, he went
down to the stable, and inquired more particularly
in relation to Joe's house.

When he had received such directions as would
enable him to find the place, he told Abner he wanted
to be absent a little while, and left the stable.   He
had no difficulty in finding the home of the drunk‑
ard's family.   It was a little, old wooden house, in
Avery Street, opposite Haymarket Place, which has
long since been pulled down, to make room for a
more elegant dwelling.

Harry knocked, and was admitted by the little .ame girl whom he had seen at the stable.

"I have come to see if I can do any thing for you," said Harry, as he moved forward into the room in which the family lived.

"Have you seen any thing of father?" asked the little girl.

"I haven't; Abner says he hasn't been to the stable to-day. Haven't you any lights?" asked Harry, as he entered the dark room.

"We haven't got any oil, nor any candles."

In the fireplace, a piece of pine board was blazing, which cast a faint and fitful glare into the room; and Harry was thus enabled to behold the scene which the miserable home of the drunkard presented.

In one corner was a dilapidated bedstead, on which lay the sick woman. Drawn from under it was a trundle bed, upon which lay two small children, who had evidently been put to bed at that early hour to keep them warm, for the temperature of the apartment was scarcely more comfortable than that of the open air. It was a cheerless home; and the faint light of the blazing board served only to increase the desolate appearance of the place.

"Who is it?" asked the sick woman, faintly.

"The boy that works at the stable," replied the lame girl.

"My name is Harry West, marm; and I come to see if you wanted any thing," added Harry.

"We want a great many things," sighed she. "Can you tell me where my husband is?"

"I can't; he hasn't been at the stable to-day."

"O God! what will become of us?" sobbed the woman.

"I will help you, marm. Don't take on so. I have money; and I will do every thing I can for you."

When her mother sobbed, the lame girl sat down on the bed, and cried bitterly. Harry's tender heart was melted; and he would have wept also, if he had not been conscious of the high mission he had to perform; and he felt very grateful that he was able to dry up those tears, and carry gladness to those bleeding hearts.

"I don't know what you can do for us," said the

poor woman, "though I am sure I am very much obliged to you."

" I can do a great deal, marm. Cheer up," replied Harry, tenderly.

As he spoke, one of the children in the trundle bed sobbed in its sleep; and the poor mother's heart seemed to be lacerated by the sound.

" Poor child!" wailed she. " He had no supper but a crust of bread and a cup of cold water. He cried himself to sleep with cold and hunger. O Heaven! that we should have come to this!"

" And the room is very cold," added Harry, glancing around him.

" It is. Our wood is all gone but two great logs. Katy could not bring them up."

" I worked for an hour trying to split some pieces off them," said Katy, the lame girl.

" I will fix them, marm," replied Harry, who felt the strength of ten stout men in his limbs at that moment. " But you have had no supper."

" No."

" Wait a minute. Have you a basket?"

Katy brought him a peck basket, and Harry rushed

out of the house as though he had been shot. Great deeds were before him, and he was inspired for the occasion.

In a quarter of an hour he returned. The basket was nearly full. Placing it in a chair, he took from it a package of candles, one of which he lighted and placed in a tin candlestick on the table.

"Now we have got a little light on the subject," said he, as he began to display the contents of the basket. "Here, Katy, is two pounds of meat; here is half a pound of tea; you had better put a little in the teapot, and let it be steeping for your mother."

"God bless you!" exclaimed Mrs. Flint. "You are an angel sent from Heaven to help us in our distress."

"No, marm; I ain't an angel," answered Harry, who seemed to feel that Julia Bryant had an exclusive monopoly of that appellation, so far as it could be reasonably applied to mortals. "I only want to do my duty, marm."

"Katy Flint was so bewildered that she could say nothing, though her opinion undoubtedly coincided with that of her mother.

"Here is two loaves of bread and two dozen crackers; a pound of butter; two pounds of sugar There! I did not bring any milk."

"Never mind the milk. You are a blessed child."

"Give me a pitcher, Katy. I will go down to Thomas's in two shakes of a jiffy."

Mrs. Flint protested that she did not want any milk — that she could get along very well without it; but Harry said the children must have it; and, without waiting for Katy to get the pitcher, he took it from the closet, and ran out of the house.

He was gone but a few minutes. When he returned, he found Katy trying to make the teakettle boil, but with very poor success.

"Now, Katy, show me the logs, and I will soon have a fire."

The lame girl conducted him to the cellar, where Harry found the remnants of the old box which Katy had tried to split. Seizing the axe, he struck a few vigorous blows, and the pine boards were reduced to a proper shape for use. Taking an armful, he returned to the chamber; and soon a good fire was blazing under the teakettle.

"There, marm, we will soon have things to rights,' said Harry, as he rose from the hearth, where he had stooped down to blow the fire.

"I am sure we should have perished if you had not come," added Mrs. Flint, who was not disposed to undervalue Harry's good deeds.

"Then I am very glad I come."

"I hope we shall be able to pay you back all the money you have spent; but I don't know. Joseph has got so bad, I don't know what he is coming to. He is a good-hearted man.   He always uses me well, even when he is in liquor.   Nothing but drink could make him neglect us so."

"It is a hard case, marm," added Harry.

"Very hard; he hasn't done much of any thing for us this winter. I have been out to work every day till a fortnight ago, when I got sick, and couldn't do any thing.   Katy has kept us alive since then; she is a good girl, and takes the whole care of Tommy and Susan."

"Poor girl! it is a pity she is so lame."

"I don't mind that, if I only had things to do with," said Katy, who was busy disposing of the provision which Harry had bought.

As soon as the kettle boiled, she made tea, an prepared a little toast for her mother, who, however, was too sick to take much nourishment.

"Now, Katy, you must eat yourself," interposed Harry, when all was ready.

" I can't eat," replied the poor girl, bursting into tears.   " I don't feel hungry."

" You must eat."

Just then the children in the trundle bed, disturbed by the unusual bustle in the room, waked, and gazed with wonder at Harry, who had seated himself on the bed.

" Poor Susy!" exclaimed Katy; " she has waked up.   And Tommy, too!   They shall have their supper, now."

They were taken up; and Harry's eyes were gladdened by such a sight as he had never beheld before. The hungry ate; and every mouthful they took swelled the heart of the little almoner of God's bounty.   If the thought of Julia Bryant, languishing on a bed of sickness, had not marred his satisfaction, he had been perfectly happy.   But he was doing a deed that would rejoice her heart; he was doing just what she had done for him ; he was doing just what she would have done, if she had been there.

"She hoped he would be a good boy." His conscience told him he had been a good boy — that he had been true to himself, and true to the noble example she had set before him.

While the family were still at supper, Harry, lighting another candle, went down cellar to pay his respects to those big logs. He was a stout boy, and accustomed to the use of the axe. By slow degrees he chipped off the logs, until they were used up, and a great pile of serviceable wood was before him. Not content with this, he carried up several large armfuls of it, which he deposited by the fireplace in the room

"Now, marm, I don't know as I can do any thing more for you to-night," said he, moving towards the door.

"The Lord knows you have done enough," replied the poor woman. "I hope we shall be able to pay you for what you have done."

"I don't want any thing, marm."

"If we can't pay you, the Lord will reward you."

"I am paid enough already. I hope you will get better, marm."

" I hope so. I feel better to-night than I have felt before for a week."

" Good night, marm! Good night, Katy!" And Harry hurried back to the stable.

" Where have you been, Harry?" asked Abner, when he entered the ostler's room.

" I have been out a little while."

" I know that. The old man wanted you; and when he couldn't find you, he was as mad as thunder."

" Where is he?" said Harry, somewhat annoyed to find that, while he had been doing his duty in one direction, he had neglected his duty in another.

" In the counting room. You will catch fits for going off."

Whatever he should catch, he determined to " face the music," and left the room to find his employer.

17

CHAPTER XV.

IN WHICH HARRY MAKES THE ACQUAINTANCE OF A VERY IMPORTANT PERSONAGE.

MAJOR PHILLIPS was in the counting room, where Harry, dreading his anger, presented himself before him. His employer was a violent man. He usually acted first, and thought the matter over afterwards; so that he frequently had occasion to undo what had been done in haste and passion. His heart was kind, but his temper generally had the first word.

"So you have come, Harry," exclaimed he, as our hero opened the door. "Where have you been?"

"I have been out a little while," replied Harry, whose modesty rebelled at the idea of proclaiming the good deed he had done.

"Out a little while!" roared the major, with an oath that froze the boy's blood. "That is enough —

enough, sir. You know I don't allow man or boy to leave the stable without letting me know it."

" I was wrong, sir ; but I —— "

" You little snivelling monkey, how dared you leave the stable ? " continued the stable keeper, heedless of the boy's submission. " I'll teach you better than that."

" Will you ? " said Harry, suddenly changing his tone, as his blood began to boil. " You can begin as quick as you like."

" You saucy young cub ! I have a great mind to give you a cowhiding," thundered the enraged stable keeper.

" I should like to see you do it," replied Harry, fixing his eyes on the poker that lay on the floor near the stove.

" Should you, you impertinent puppy ? "

The major sprang forward, as if to grasp the boy by the collar ; but Harry, with his eye still fixed on the poker, retreated a pace or two, ready to act promptly when the decisive moment should come. Forgetting for the time that he had run away from one duty to attend to another, he felt indignant that

he should be thus rudely treated for being absent a
short time on an errand of love and charity. He
gave himself too much credit for the good deed, and
felt that he was a martyr to his philanthropic spirit.
He was willing to bear all and brave all in a good
cause; and it seemed to him, just then, as though
he was being punished for assisting Joe Flint's family, instead of for leaving his place without permission. A great many persons who mean well are apt
to think themselves martyrs for any good cause in
which they may be engaged, when, in reality, their
own want of tact, or the offensive manner in which
they present their truth, is the stake at which they
are burned.

"Keep off!" said Harry, his eyes flashing fire.

The major was so angry that he could do nothing;
and while they were thus confronting each other, Joe
Flint staggered into the counting room. Intoxicated
as he was, he readily discovered the position of affairs
between the belligerents.

"Look here — hic — Major Phillips," said he,
reeling up to his employer, "I love you, — hic, —
Major Phillips, like a — hic — like a brother, Major

Phillips; but if you touch that boy, Major Phillips. I'll — hic — you touch me, Major Phillips. That's all."

"Go home, Joe," replied the stable keeper, his attention diverted from Harry to the new combatant. "You are drunk."

"I know I'm drunk, Major Phillips. I'm as drunk as a beast; but I ain't — hic — dead drunk. I know what I'm about."

"No, you don't. Go home."

"Yes, I dzoo. I'm a brute; I'm a hog; I'm a — dzwhat you call it? I'm a villain."

Joe tried to straighten himself up, and look at his employer; but he could not, and suddenly bursting into tears, he threw himself heavily into a chair, weeping bitterly in his inebriate paroxysm. He sobbed, and groaned, and talked incoherently. He acted strangely, and Major Phillips's attention was excited.

"What is the matter, Joe?" he asked; and his anger towards Harry seemed to have subsided.

"I tell you I am a villain, Major Phillips," blubbered Joe.

17 *

" What do you mean by that?"

" Haven't I been on a drunk, and left my family to starve and freeze?" groaned Joe, interlarding his speech with violent ebullitions of weeping. " Wouldn't my poor wife, and my poor children — O my God!" and the poor drunkard covered his face with his hands, and sobbed like an infant.

" What is the matter? What do you mean, Joe?" asked Major Phillips, who had never seen him in this frame before. .

" Wouldn't they all have died, if Harry hadn't gone and fed 'em, and split up wood to warm 'em?"

As he spoke, Joe sprang up, and rushed towards Harry, and in his drunken frenzy attempted to embrace him.

" What does this mean, Harry?" said the stable keeper, turning to our hero, who, while Joe was telling his story, had been thinking of something else.

" What a fool I was to get mad!" thought he. 'What would she say, if she had seen me just now? Poor Julia! perhaps she is dead, even now."

" My folks would have died, if it hadn't b' en for him," hiccoughed Joe.

"Explain it, Harry," added the major.

"The lame girl, Katy, came down here after her father, early in the evening. She seemed to be in trouble, and I thought I would go up and see what the matter was. I found them in rather a bad condition, without any wood or any thing to eat. I did what I could for them, and came away," replied Harry.

"Give me your hand, Harry! ' 'and the major grasped his hand like a vice. "You are a good fellow," he added, with an oath.

"Forgive me, Mr. Phillips, for saying what I did; I was mad," pleaded Harry.

"So was I, my boy; but we won't mind that. You are a good fellow; and I like your spunk. So you have really been taking care of Joe's family while he was off on a drunk."

"I didn't do much, sir."

"Look here, Harry, and you, Major Phillips When I get this rum out of me, I'll never take another drop again," said Joe, throwing himself into a chair.

"Bah, Joe! You have said that twenty times before," added Major Phillips.

" You dzee !" exclaimed Joe, doubling his fist, and bringing it down with the intention of hitting the table by his side to emphasize his resolution; but, unfortunately, he missed the table — a circumstance which seemed to foreshadow the fate of his resolve.

Joe proceeded to declare in his broken speech what a shock he had received when he went home, half an hour before, — the first time for several days, — and heard the reproaches of his suffering wife, how grateful he was to Harry, and what a villain he considered himself. Either the sufferings of his family, or the rum he had drank, melted his heart, and he was as eloquent as his half-paralyzed tongue would permit. He was a pitiable object; and having assured himself that Joe's family were comfortable for the night, Major Phillips put him to bed in his own house.

Harry was not satisfied with himself; he had permitted his temper to get the better of him. He thought of Julia on her bed of suffering, wept for her, and repented for himself. That night he heard the clock on the Boylston market strike twelve before he closed his eyes to sleep.

The next day, while he was at work in the stable, a boy of about fifteen called to see him, and desired to speak with him alone. Harry, much wondering who his visitor was, and what he wanted, conducted him to the ostler's chamber.

" You are Harry West," the boy began.

" That is my name, for the want of a better," replied Harry.

" Then there is a little matter to be settled between you and me. You helped my folks out last night, and I want to pay you for it."

" Your folks ? "

" My name is Edward Flint."

" Then you are Joe's son."

" I am," replied Edward, who did not seem to feel much honored by the relationship.

" Your folks were in a bad condition last night."

" That's a fact; they were."

" But I didn't know Joe had a son as old as you are."

" I am the oldest; but I don't live at home, and have not for three years. How much did you pay out for them last night ? "

" One dollar and twenty cents."

" As much as that ? "

" Just that."

Edward Flint manifested some uneasiness at the announcement. He had evidently come with a pur‑ pose, but had found things different from what he had expected.

" I didn't think it was so much."

" What matter how much ? " asked Harry

" Why, I want to pay you."

" You needn't mind that."

" The fact is, I have only three dollars just now; and I promised to go out to ride with a fellow next Sunday. So, you see, if I pay you, I shall not have enough left to foot the bills."

Harry looked at his visitor with astonishment; he did not know what to make of him. Was he in earnest? Would a son of Joseph Flint go out to ride, — on Sunday, too, — while his mother and his brother and sisters were on the very brink of starva‑ tion? Our hero had some strange, old‑fashioned notions of his own. For instance, he considered it a son's duty to take care of his mother, even if he

were obliged to forego the Sunday ride; that he
ought to do all he could for his brothers and sisters,
even if he had to go without stewed oysters, stay
away from the theatre, and perhaps wear a little
coarser cloth on his back. If Harry was unreasonable in his views, my young reader will remember that
he was brought up in the country, where young
America is not quite so " fast·" as in the city.

" I didn't ask you to pay me," continued Harry.

" I know that; but, you see, I suppose I ought to
pay you. The old man don't take much care of the
family."

Harry wanted to say that the young man did not
appear to do much better; but he was disposed to
be as civil as the circumstances would permit.

" You needn't pay me."

" O, yes, I shall pay you; but if you can wait till
the first of next month, I shou.d like it."

" I can wait. Do you live out?"

" Live out? What do you mean by that? I am
a clerk in a store down town," replied Edward with
offended dignity.

" O, are you? Do they pay you well?"

" Pretty fair; I get five dollars a week."

" Five dollars a week! Thunder! I should think you did get paid pretty well!" exclaimed Harry, astonished at the vastness of the sum for a week's work.

" Fair salary," added Edward, complacently. " What are you doing here?"

" I work in the stable and about the house."

" That's mean business," said Mr. Flint, turning up his nose.

" It does very well."

" How much do you get?'

" Six dollars a month and perquisites."

" How much are the perquisites?"

" From one to two dollars a month."

" Humph! I wonder you stay here."

" It is as well as I can do."

" No, it isn't; why don't you go into a store We want a boy in our store."

" Do you?"

" We do."

" How much do you pay?"

" We pay from two to four dollars a week."

"Can't you get me the place?" asked Harry, now much interested in his companion.

"Well, yes; perhaps I can."

"What should I have to do?"

"Make the fires, sweep out in the morning, go of errands, and such work. Boys must begin at the foot of the ladder. I began at the foot of the ladder," answered Mr. Flint, with an immense self-sufficiency, which Harry, however, failed to notice.

"I should like to get into a store."

"You would have a good chance to rise."

"I am willing to do any thing, so that I can have a chance to get ahead."

"We always give boys a good chance."

Harry wanted that mysterious "we" defined. As it was, he was left to infer that Mr. Flint was a partner in the concern, unless the five dollars per week was an argument to the contrary; but he didn't like to ask strange questions, and desired to know whom "he worked for."

Edward Flint did not "work for" any body. He was a clerk in the extensive dry goods establishment of the Messrs. Wake and Wade, which, he declared,

18

was the largest concern in Boston; and one might further have concluded that Mr. Flint was the most important personage in the said concern.

Mr. Flint was obliged to descend from his lofty dignity, and compound the dollar and twenty cents with the stable boy by promising to get him the vacant place in the establishment of Wake and Wade, if his influence was sufficient to procure it. Harry was satisfied, and begged him not to distress himself about the debt. The visitor took his leave, promising to see him again the next day.

About noon, Joe Flint appeared at the stable again, perfectly sober. Major Phillips had lent him ten dollars, in anticipation of his month's wages, and he had been home to attend to the comfort of his suffering family. After dinner, he had a long talk with Harry, in which, after paying him the money disbursed on the previous evening, he repeated his solemn resolution to drink no more. He was very grateful to Harry, and hoped he should be able to do as much for him.

" Don't drink any more, Joe, and it will be the best day's work I ever did," added Harry.

" I never will, Harry — never! ' protested Joe.

CHAPTER XVI.

IN WHICH HARRY GOES INTO THE DRY GOODS
BUSINESS.

MR. EDWARD FLINT's reputation as a gentleman of honor and a man of his word suffered somewhat in Harry's estimation; for he waited all day, and all the evening, without hearing a word from the firm of Wake and Wade. He had actually begun to doubt whether the accomplished young man had as much influence with the firm as he had led him to suppose. But his ambition would not permit him longer to be satisfied with the humble sphere of a stable boy; and he determined, if he did not hear from Edward, to apply for the situation himself.

The next day, having procured two hours' leave of absence from the stable, he called at the home of Joe Flint to obtain further particulars concerning Edward and his situation. He found the family in

much better circumstances than at his previous visit.
Mrs. Flint was sitting up, and was rapidly convalescing; Katy was busy and cheerful; and it seemed
a different place from that to which he had been the
messenger of hope and comfort two nights before.

They were very glad to see him, and poured forth
their gratitude to him so eloquently that he was obliged
to change the topic. Mrs. Flint was sure that her
husband was an altered man. She had never before
known him to be so earnest and solemn in his resolutions to amend and lead a new life.

But when Harry alluded to Edward, both Katy
and her mother suddenly grew sad. They acknowledged that they had sent for him in their extremity,
out that he did not come till the next morning, when
the bounty of the stable boy had relieved them from
the bitterness of want. The mother dropped a tear
as she spoke of the wayward son; and Harry had
not the heart to press the inquiries he had come to
make.

After speaking as well as he dared to speak of
Edward, he took his leave, and hastened to the establishment of Wake and Wade, to apply for the vacant

place. He had put on his best clothes, and his appearance this time was very creditable.

Entering the store, he inquired for Edward Flint; and that gentleman was summoned to receive him.

"Hallo, Harry West!" said Edward, when he recognized his visitor. "I declare I forgot all about you."

"I thought likely," replied Harry, willing to be very charitable to the delinquent.

"The fact is, we have been so busy in the store, I haven't had time to call on you, as I promised."

"Never mind, now. Is the place filled?"

"No."

"I am glad to hear that. Do you think there is any chance for me?"

"Well, I don't know. I will do what I can for you."

"Thank you, Edward."

"Wait here a moment till I speak with one of the partners."

The clerk left him, and was absent but a moment, when Harry was summoned to the private room of Mr Wake. The gentleman questioned him for a

18 *

few moments, and seemed to be pleased with his address and his frankness. The result of the interview was, that our hero was engaged at a salary of three dollars a week, though it was objected to him that he had no parents residing in the city.

" I thought I could fix it," said Edward, complacently, as they left the counting room.

" I am much obliged to you, Edward," replied Harry, willing to humor his new friend. "**Now I** want to get a place to board."

" That is easy enough."

" Where do you board?"

" In Green Street."

" How much do you **pay a week?**"

" Two dollars and a half."

" I can't pay that."

" Well, I suppose you can't."

" I was thinking of something just now.   Suppose we should both board with **your** mother."

" Me?"

" Yes."

" What, in a ten-footer!" exclaimed Edward, starting back with astonishment and indignation at the proposal.

" Why not? If it is good enough for your mother, isn't it good enough for you ? "

" Humph ! I'll bet it won't suit me."

" We can fix up a room to suit ourselves, you know. And it will be much cheaper for both of us."

" That, indeed ; but the idea of boarding with the old man is not to be thought of."

" I should think you would like to be with your mother and your brother and sisters."

" Not particular about it."

" Better think of it, Edward."

The clerk promised to think about it, but did not consider it very probable that he should agree to the proposition.

Harry returned to the stable, and immediately notified Major Phillips of his intention to leave his service As may be supposed, the stable keeper was sorry to lose him ; but he did not wish to stand in the way of his advancement. He paid him his wages, adding a gift of five dollars, and kindly permitted him to leave at once, as he desired to procure a place to board, and to acquaint himself with the localities of the city, so that he could discharge his duty the more acceptably to his new employers.

The ostlers, too, were sorry to part with him --
particularly Joe Flint, whose admiration of our hero
was unbounded. In their rough and honest hearts
they wished him well. They had often made fun of
his good principles; often laughed at him for refusing to pitch cents in the back yard on Sunday,
and for going to church instead; often ridiculed him
under the name of " Little Pious ; " still they had a
great respect for him. They who are "persecuted
for righteousness' sake " — who are made fun of
because they strive to do right — are always sure of
the victory in the end. They may be often tried, but
sooner or later they shall triumph.

After dinner, he paid another visit to Mrs. Flint,
in Avery Street. He opened his proposition to board
in her family, to which she raised several objections,
the chief of which was, that she had no room. The
plan was more favorably received by Katy ; and she
suggested that they could hire the little apartment
up stairs, which was used as a kind of lumber room
by the family in the other part of the house.

Her mother finally consented to the arrangement,
and it became necessary to decide upon the terms

for Harry was a prudent manager, and left nothing to
be settled afterwards. He then introduced the project he had mentioned to Edward; and Mrs. Flint
thought she could board them both for three dollars
a week, if they could put up with humble fare.
Harry declared that he was not "difficult," though
he could not speak for Edward.

Our hero was delighted with the success of his
scheme, and only wished that Edward had consented
to the arrangement; but the next time he saw him,
somewhat to his surprise, the clerk withdrew his
objections, and entered heartily into the scheme.

"You see, Harry, I shall make a dollar a week —
fifty-two dollars a year — by the arrangement," said
Edward, after he had consented.

He evidently considered that some apology was
due from him for descending from the social dignity
of his position in the Green Street boarding house
to the humble place beneath his mother's roof.

"Certainly you will; and that is a great deal of
money," replied Harry.

"It will pay my theatre tickets, and for a ride
once a month besides."

"For what?" asked Harry, astonished at his companion's theory of economy.

Edward repeated his statement.

"Why don't you save your money?"

"Save it? What is the use of that? I mean to have a good time while I can."

"You never will be a rich man."

"I'll bet I will."

"You could give your mother and Katy a great many nice things with that money."

"Humph! The old man must take care of them. It is all I can do to take care of myself."

"If I had a mother, and brothers and sisters, I should be glad to spend all I got in making them nappy," sighed Harry.

On the following Monday morning, Harry went to his new place. He was in a strange position. All was untried and unfamiliar. Even the language of the clerks and salesmen was strange to him; and he was painfully conscious of the deficiencies of his education and of his knowledge of business. He was prompt, active, and zealous; yet his awkwardness could not be concealed. The transition from the stable to the store was as great as from a hovel to a palace. He made a great many blunders. Mr. Wake laughed at him; Mr. Wade swore at him; and all the clerks made him the butt of their mirth or their ill nature, just as they happened to feel.

What seemed to him worse than all, Edward Flint joined the popular side, and laughed and swore with the rest. Poor Harry was almost discouraged before dinner time, and began very seriously to consider whether he had not entirely mistaken his calling. Dinner, however, seemed to inspire him with new courage and new energy; and he hastened back to the store, resolved to try again.

The shop was crowded with customers; and partners and clerks hallooed "Harry" till he was so confused that he hardly knew whether he stood on his head or his heels. It was, Come here, Go there, Bring this, Bring that; but in spite of laugh and curse, of push and kick, he persevered, suiting nobody, least of all himself.

It was a long day, a very long day; but it came to an end at last. Our hero had hardly strength enough left to put up the shutters. His legs ached

his head ached, and, worse than all, his heart ached
at the manifest failure of his best intentions. He
thought of going to the partners, and asking them
whether they thought he was fit for the place ; but
he finally decided to try again for another day, and
dragged himself home to rest his weary limbs.

He and Edward had taken possession of their room
at Joe Flint's house that morning ; and on their
arrival, they found that Katy had put every thing in
excellent order for their reception. Harry was too
much fatigued and disheartened to have a very lively
appreciation of the comforts of his new home ; but
Edward, notwithstanding the descent he had made,
was in high spirits. He even declared that the room
they were to occupy was better than his late apart·
ment in Green Street.

" Do you think I shall get along with my work,
Edward ? " asked Harry, gloomily, after they had
gone to bed.

" Why not ? "

" Every body in the store has kicked and cuffed
me, swore at and abused me, till I feel like a jelly."

" O, never mind that ; they always do so with a

green one. They served me just so when I first went into business."

" Did they? "

" Fact. One must live and learn."

" It seemed to me just as though I never could suit them."

" Pooh? Don't be blue about it."

" I can't help it. I know I did not suit them."

" Yes, you did."

" What made them laugh at me and swear at me, then? "

" That is the fashion; you must talk right up to them. If they swear at you, swear at them back again — that is, at the clerks and salesmen. If they give you any 'lip,' let 'em have as good as they send."

" I don't want to do that."

" Must do it, Harry. 'Live and learn' is my motto. When you go among the Romans, do as the Romans do."

Harry did not like this advice; for he who, among the Romans, would do as the Romans do, among hogs would do as the hogs do.

" If I only suit them, I don't care."

" You do; I heard Wake tell Wade that you were a first rate boy."

" Did you ? "   And Harry's heart swelled with joy to think that, in spite of his trials, he had actually triumphed in the midst of them.

So he dropped the subject, with the resolution to redouble his exertions to please his employers the next day, and turned his thoughts to Julia Bryant, to wonder if she were still living, or had become an angel indeed.

CHAPTER XVII.

IN WHICH HARRY REVISITS ROCKVILLE, AND MEETS WITH A SERIOUS LOSS.

THE next evening, Harry was conscious of having gained a little in the ability to discharge his nove' duties. Either the partners and the clerks had become tired of swearing and laughing at him, or he had made a decided improvement; for less fault was found with him, and his position was much more satisfactory. With a light heart he put up the shutters; for though he was very much fatigued, the prestige of future success was so cheering, that he scarcely heeded his weary, aching limbs.

Every day was an improvement on the preceding day, and before the week was out, Harry found himself quite at home in his new occupation. He was never a moment behind the time at which he was required to be at the store in the morning. This promptness was specially noted by the partners; for when they came to their business in the morning, they found the store well warmed, the floor nicely swept, and every thing put in order.

When he was sent out with bundles, he did not stop to look at the pictures in the shop windows, to play marbles, or tell long stories to other boys in the streets. If his employers had even been very unreasonable, they could not have helped being pleased with the new boy, and Wake confidentially assured Wade that they had got a treasure.

Our hero was wholly devoted to his business. He intended to make a man of himself, and he could only accomplish his purpose by constant exertion, by constant study, and constant "trying again." He was obliged to keep a close watch over himself, for often he was tempted to be idle and negligent, to be careless and indifferent.

After supper, on Thursday evening of his second week at Wake and Wade's, he hastened to Major Phillips' stable to see John Lane, and obtain the news from Rockville. His heart beat violently when he saw John's great wagon, for he dreaded some fearful announcement from his sick friend. He had not before been so deeply conscious of his indebtedness to the little angel, as now, when she lay upon the bed of pain, perhaps of death. She had kindled in his soul a love for the good and the beautiful. She had inspired him with a knowledge of the difference between the right and the wrong. In a word, she was the guiding star of his existence. Her approbation was to be the bright guerdon of fidelity to truth and principle.

"How is Julia?" asked Harry, without giving John time to inquire why he had left the stable.

"They think she is a little grain better."

"Then she is still living?" continued Harry, a great load of anxiety removed from his soul.

"She is; but it is very doubtful how it will turn I went in to see her yesterday, and she spoke of you."

"Spoke of me?"

"She said she should like to see you."

"I should like to see her very much."

"Her father told me, if you was a mind to go up to Rockville, he would pay your expenses."

"I don't mind the expenses. I will go, if I can get away."

"Her father feels very bad about it. Julia is an only child, and he would do any thing in the world to please her."

" I will go and see the gentlemen I work for, and if they will let me, I will go with you to-morrow morning."

" Better take the stage; you will get there so much quicker."

" I will do so, then."

Harry returned home to ascertain of Edward where Mr. Wake lived, and hastened to see him. That gentleman, however, coldly assured him, if he went to Rockville, he must lose his place — they could not get along without a boy. In vain Harry urged that he should be gone but two days; the senior was inflexible.

" What shall I do ? " said he to himself, when he got into the street again. "Mr. Wake says, she is no relation of mine, and he don't see why I should go. Poor Julia! She may die, and I shall never see her again. I must go."

It did not require a great deal of deliberation to convince himself that it was his duty to visit the sick girl. She had been a true friend to him, and he could afford to sacrifice his place to procure her even a slight gratification. Affection and duty called him one way, self-interest the other. If he did not go, he should regret it as long as he lived. Perhaps Mr. Wake would take him again on his return; if not, he could at least go to work in the stable again.

" Edward, I am going to Rockville to-morrow," he remarked to his " chum," on his return to Mrs. Flint's.

" The old man agreed to it, then? I thought he wouldn't. He never will let a fellow off even for a day."

" He did not; but I must go."

" Better not, then. He will discharge you, for he is a hard nut "

" I must go," repeated Harry, taking a candle, and going up to their chamber.

" You have got more spunk than I gave you credit for; but you are sure of losing your place," replied Edward, following him up stairs.

" I can't help it."

Harry opened a drawer in the old broken bureau in the room, and from beneath his clothes took out the great pill box which served him for a savings bank

" You have got lots of money," remarked Edward, as he glanced at the contents of the box.

" Not much ; only twelve dollars," replied Harry, taking out three of them to pay his expenses to Rockville.

" You won't leave that box there, will you, while you are gone ? "

" Why not ? "

" Somebody may steal it."

" I guess not.   I can hide it, though, before I go."

" Better do so."

Harry took his money and went to a bookstore in Washington Street, where he purchased an appropri· ate present for Julia, for which he gave half a dollar. On his return, he wrote her name in it, with his own as the giver.   Then the safety of his money came up for consideration ; and this matter was settled by raising a loose board in the floor, and depositing the

pill box in a secure place. He had scarcely done so
before Edward joined him.

Our hero did not sleep much that night. He was
not altogether satisfied with the step he was about to
take. It was not doing right by his employers; but
he compromised the matter in part by engaging Edward, "for a consideration," to make the fires and
sweep out the next morning.

At noon, on the following day, he reached Rockville, and hastened to the house of Mr. Bryant.

"How is she?" he asked, breathless with interest,
of the girl who answered his knock.

"She is better to-day. Are you the boy from
Boston?"

"Yes. Do they think she will get well?"

"The doctor has more hope of her."

"I am very glad to hear it."

Harry was conducted into the house, and Mr. Bryant was informed of his presence.

"I am glad you have come, Harry. Julia is much
better to-day," said her father, taking him by the
hand "She has frequently spoken of you, during
her illness, and feels a very strong interest in your
welfare."

"She was very good to me. I don't know what would have become of me if she had not been a friend to me."

"That is the secret of her interest in you. We love those best whom we serve most. She is asleep now; but you shall see her as soon as she wakes. In the mean time you had better have your dinner.

Mr. Bryant looked very pale, and his eyes were reddened with weeping. Harry saw how much he nad suffered during the last fortnight; but it seemed natural to him that he should suffer terribly at the thought of losing one so beautiful and precious as the little angel.

He dined alone with Mr. Bryant, for Mrs. Bryant could not leave the couch of the little sufferer. The fond father could speak of nothing but Julia, and more than once the tears flooded his eyes, as he told Harry how meek and patient she had been through the fever, how loving she was, and how resigned even to leave her parents, and go to the heavenly Parent, to dwell with him forever.

Harry wept, too; and after dinner, he almost feared to enter the chamber, and behold the wreck which disease had made of that bright and beautiful form. Removing the wrapper from the book he had brought, — a volume of sweet poems, entitled " Angel Songs," — he followed Mr. Bryant into the sick girl's chamber.

" Ah, Harry, I am delighted to see you!" exclaimed she, in a whisper, for her diseased throat rendered articulation difficult and painful.

" I am sorry to see you so sick, Julia," replied Harry, taking the wasted hand she extended to him.

" I am better, Harry. I feel as though I should get well now."

" I hope you will."

" You don't know how much I have thought of you, while I lay here ; how I wished you were my brother, and could come in every day and see me," she continued, with a faint smile.

" I wish I could."

" Now tell me how you get along in Boston."

" Very well; but your father says I must not talk much with you now. I have brought you a little book ; " and he placed it in her hand.

" How good you are, Harry ! 'Angel Songs.

How pretty! Now, Harry, you must read me one of the angel songs."

" I will ; but I can't read very well," said he, as he opened the volume.

But he did read exceedingly well. The piece he selected was a very pretty and a very touching little song ; and Harry's feelings were so deeply moved by the pathetic sentiments of the poem and their adaptation to the circumstances of the case, that he was quite eloquent.

When he had finished, Mrs. Bryant interfered to prevent further conversation ; and Julia, though she had a great deal to say to her young friend, cheerfully yielded to her mother's wishes, and Harry reluctantly left the room.

Towards night he was permitted to see her again, when he read several of the angel songs to her, and gave her a brief account of the events of his residence in Boston. She was pleased with his earnestness, and smiled approvingly upon him for the moral triumphs he had achieved. The reward of all his struggles with trial and temptation was lavishly bestowed in her commendation, and if fidelity had not been its own reward, he could have accepted her approval as abundant compensation for all he had endured. There was no silly sentiment in Harry's composition; he had read no novels, seen no plays, knew nothing of romance even " in real life." The homage he yielded to the fair and loving girl was an unaffected reverence for simple purity and goodness; that which the True Heart and the True Life never fail to call forth wherever they exert their power.

On the following morning, Julia's condition was very much improved, and the physician spoke confidently of a favorable issue. Harry was permitted to pend an hour by her bedside, inhaling the pure spirit that pervaded the soul of the sick one. She was so much better that her father proposed to visit the city, to attend to some urgent business, which had been long deferred by her illness; and an opportunity was thus afforded for Harry to return.

Mr. Bryant drove furiously in his haste, changing horses twice on the journey, so that they reached the city at one o'clock. On their arrival, Harry's attention naturally turned to the reception he expected to receive from his employers. He had not spoken of his relations with them at Rockville, preferring not to pain them, on the one hand, and not to take too much credit to himself for his devotion to Julia, on the other. After the horse was disposed of at Major Phillips's stable, Mr. Bryant walked down town with Harry; and when they reached the store of Wake and Wade, he entered with him.

"What have you come back for?" asked the senior partner, rather coldly, when he saw the delinquent. "We don't want you."

Harry was confused at this reception, though it was not unexpected.

"I didn't know but that you might be willing to take me again."

"No, we don't want you. Ah, Mr. Bryant? Happy to see you," continued Mr. Wake, recognizing Harry's friend.

"Did I understand you aright? Did you say that you did not want my young friend, here?" replied Mr. Bryant, taking the offered hand of Mr. Wake.

"I did say so," said the senior. "I was not aware that he was your friend, though;" and he proceeded to inform Mr. Bryant. that Harry had left them against their wish.

"A few words with you, if you please."

Mr. Wake conducted him to the private office, where they remained for half an hour.

"It is all right, Harry," continued Mr. Wake, on their return. "I did not understand the matter."

"Thank you, sir!" ejaculated our hero, rejoiced to find his place was still secure. "I would no* have gone if I could possibly have helped it."

"You did right, my boy, and I honor you for your courage and constancy."

Mr. Bryant bade him an affectionate adieu, promising to write to him often until Julia recovered, and then departed.

With a grateful heart Harry immediately resumed his duties, and the partners were probably as glad to retain him as he was to remain.

At night, when he went to his chamber, he raised the loose board to get the pill box, containing his savings, in order to return the money he had not expended. To his consternation, he discovered that it was gone!

CHAPTER XVIII.

IN WHICH HARRY MEETS WITH AN OLD AC-
QUAINTANCE, AND GETS A HARD KNOCK ON
THE. HEAD.

It was in vain that Harry searched beneath the
broken floor for his lost treasure; it could not be
found. He raised the boards up, and satisfied himself that it had not slipped away into any crevice, or
fallen through into the room below; and the conclusion was inevitable that the box had been stolen.

Who could have stolen it? The mystery confused
Harry; for he was certain that no one had seen him
deposit the box beneath the floor. No one except
Edward even knew that he had any money. He was
sure that neither Mrs. Flint nor Katy would have
stolen it; and he was not willing to believe that his
room mate would be guilty of such a mean and con-
temptible act.

He tried to assure himself that it had not been stolen — that it was still somewhere beneath the floor; and he pulled up another board, to resume the search. He had scarcely done so before Edward joined him.

" What are you about, Harry ? " he asked, apparently very much astonished at his chum's occupation " Are you going to pull the house down ? "

" Not exactly. You know my pill box ? " replied Harry, suspending operations to watch Edward' expression when he told him of his loss.

" The one you kept your money in ? "

" Yes. Well, it is gone."

" Gone ! " exclaimed Edward, starting back with surprise.

" It is either lost or stolen."

" What did you do with it ? "

" Put it here, under this loose board."

" It must be there now, then. I will help you find it."

Edward manifested a great deal of enthusiasm in the search. He was sure it must be where Harry had put it, or that it had rolled back out of sight;

and he began tearing up the floor with a zeal that threatened the destruction of the building. But the box could not be found, and they were obliged to abandon the search.

" Too bad, Harry."

" That is a fact; I can't spare that money, any how. I have been a good while earning it, and it is too thundering bad to lose it."

" I don't understand it," continued Edward.

" Nor I either," replied Harry, looking his companion sharp in the eye. " No one knew I had it but you."

" Do you mean to say I stole it?" exclaimed Edward, doubling his fist, while his cheek reddened with anger.

" I don't say so."

" Humph! Well, you better not."

" Don't get mad, Edward. I didn't mean to lay it to you."

" Didn't you?" And Edward was very glad to have the matter compromised.

" I did not; perhaps I spoke hastily. You know how hard I worked for this money; and it seems hard to lose it. But no matter; I will try again."

M*s* Flint and Katy were much grieved when Harry told of his loss. They looked as though they suspected Edward; but they said nothing; for it was very hard to accuse a son or a brother of such a crime.

Mrs. Flint advised Harry to put his money in the savings bank in future, promising to take care of his spare funds till they amounted to five dollars, which was then the smallest sum that would be received. It was a long time before our hero became reconciled to his loss. He had made up his mind to be a rich man; and he had carefully hoarded every cent he could spare, thus closely imitating the man who got rich by saving his fourpences.

A few days after the loss, he was reading in one of Katy's Sunday school books about a miser. The wretch was held up as a warning to young folks, by showing them how he starved his body and soul for the sake of gold.

"That's why I lost my money!" exclaimed Harry as he laid the book upon the window.

"What do you mean, Harry?" asked Katy, who sat near him.

"I have been hoarding up my money just like this old man in the book."

"You are not a miser, Harry. You couldn't be mean and stingy, if you tried."

"Yes, I could. I love money."

"So does every body."

"A miser wouldn't do what you did for us, Harry," added Mrs. Flint. "We ought to be careful and saving."

"I have been thinking too much of money. After all, perhaps it was just as well that I lost that money."

"I am sorry you lost it; for I don't think there is any danger of your becoming a miser," said Katy.

"Perhaps not; at any rate, it has set me to thinking."

Harry finished the book; and it was, fortunately, just such a work as he required to give him right and proper views in regard to the value of wealth. His dream of being a rich man was essentially modified by these views; and he renewedly resolved that it was better to be a good man than to be a rich man,

If he could not be both. It seemed to him a little remarkable that the minister should preach upon this very topic on the following Sunday, taking for his text the words, "Seek ye first the kingdom of heaven, and all these things shall be added unto you." He was deeply impressed by the sermon, probably because it was on a subject to which he had given some attention.

A few days after his return from Rockville, Harry received a very cheerful letter from Mr. Bryant, to which Julia had added a few lines in a postscript. The little angel was rapidly recovering, and our hero was rejoiced beyond expression. The favorable termination of her illness was a joy which far outbalanced the loss of his money, and he was as cheerful and contented as ever. As he expressed it, in rather homely terms, he had got "the streak of fat and the streak of lean." Julia was alive; was to smile upon him again; was still to inspire him with that love of goodness which had given her such an influence over him.

Week after week passed by, and Harry heard nothing of his lost treasure; but Julia had fully recovered, and for the treasure lost an incomparably greater treasure had been gained. Edward and himself continued to occupy the same room, though ever since the loss of the money box Harry's chum had treated him coldly. There had never been much sympathy between them; for while Edward was at the theatre, or perhaps at worse places, Harry was at home, reading some good book, writing a letter to Rockville, or employed in some other worthy occupation. While Harry was at church or at the Sunday school, Edward, in company with some dissolute companion, was riding about the adjacent country.

Mrs. Flint often remonstrated with her son upon the life he led, and the dissipated habits he was contracting; and several times Harry ventured to introduce the subject. Edward, however, would not hear a word from either. It is true that we either grow better or worse, as we advance in life; and Edward Flint's path was down a headlong steep. His mother wept, and begged him to be a better boy. He only laughed at her.

Harry often wondered how he could afford to ride out, and visit the theatre and other places of amuse-

ment so frequently. His salary was only five dollars
a week now; it was only four when he had said it
was five. He seemed to have money at all times,
and to spend it very freely. He could not help be-
lieving that the contents of his pill box had paid for
some of the "stews" and "Tom and Jerrys" which
his reckless chum consumed. But the nine dollars
he had lost would have been but a drop in the bucket
compared with his extravagant outlays.

One day, about six months after Harry's return
from Rockville, as he was engaged behind the counter, a young man entered the store, and accosted him

"Halloo, Harry! How are you?"

It was a familiar voice; and, to Harry's surprise,
but not much to his satisfaction, he recognized his
old companion, Ben Smart, who, he had learned from
Mr. Bryant, had been sent to the house of correction
for burning Squire Walker's barn.

"How do you do, Ben?" returned Harry, not very
cordially.

"So you are here — are you?"

"Yes, I have been here this six months."

"Good place?"

" First rate."

" Any chance for me ? "

" No, I guess not."

" You have got a sign out for a boy, I see."

It was true they had. There were more errands
to run than one boy could attend to ; besides, Harry
had proved himself so faithful and so intelligent, that
Mr. Wake wished to retain him in the store, to fit
him for a salesman.

" You can speak a good word for me, Harry ; for
I should like to work here," continued Ben.

" I thought you were in — in the —— "

Harry did not like to use the offensive expression ;
and Ben's face darkened when he discovered what
the other was going to say.

" Not a word about that," said he. " If you ever
mention that little matter, I'll take your life."

" But how was it ? "

" My father got me out, and then I ran away. Not
a word more, for I had as lief be hung for an old
sheep as a lamb."

" There is Mr. Wake ; you can apply to him,"
continued Harry.

Ben walked boldly up to Mr. Wake, and asked for the place. The senior talked with him a few moments, and then retired to his private office, calling Harry as he entered.

"If you say any thing, I will be the death of you,' whispered Ben, as Harry passed him on his way to the office.

Our hero was not particularly pleased with these threats; he certainly was not frightened by them.

"Do you know that boy, Harry?" asked Mr. Wake, as he presented himself before the senior.

"I do, sir."

"Who is he, and what is he?"

"His name is Benjamin Smart. He belongs to Redfield."

"To Redfield? He said he came from Worcester."

"I believe Mr. Bryant told you the story about my leaving Redfield," said Harry.

"He did."

"That is the boy that run away with me."

"And the one that set the barn afire?"

"Yes, sir."

" That is enough." And Harry returned to his work at the counter.

" What did he say to you ? " asked Ben.

Before Harry had time to make any reply, Mr. Wake joined them.

" We don't want you, young man," said he.

With a glance of hatred at Harry, the applicant left the store. Since leaving Redfield, our hero's views of duty had undergone a change ; and he now realized that to screen a wicked person was to plot with him against the good order of society. He knew Ben's character ; he had no reason, after their interview, to suppose it was changed ; and he could not wrong his employers by permitting them igno- rantly to engage a bad boy, especially when he had been questioned directly on the point.

Towards evening, Harry was sent with a bundle to a place in Boylston Street, which required him to cross the Common. On his return, when he reached the corner of the burying ground, Ben Smart, who had evidently followed him, and lay in wait at this spot for him, sprang from his covert upon him. The young villain struck him a heavy blow in the eye before Harry realized his purpose. The blow, however, was vigorously returned; but Ben, besides being larger and stronger than his victim, had a large stone in his hand, with which he struck him a blow on the side of the head, knocking him insensible to the ground.

The wretch, seeing that he had done his work, fled along the side of the walk of the burying ground, pursued by several persons who had witnessed the assault. Ben was a fleet runner this time, and succeeded in making his escape.

CHAPTER XIX.

IN WHICH HARRY FINDS THAT EVEN A BROKEN
HEAD MAY BE OF SOME USE TO A PERSON.

WHEN Harry recovered his consciousness, he found
aimself in an elegantly furnished chamber, with several persons standing around the bed upon which he
had been laid.   A physician was bending over him,
engaged in dressing the severe wound he had received
in the side of his head.

"There, young man, you have had a narrow escape," said the doctor, as he saw his patient's eyes
open.

"Where am I?" asked Harry, faintly, as he tried
to concentrate his wandering senses.

"You are in good hands, my boy.   What is your
name?"

"Harry West.   Can't I go home now?" replied
.he sufferer, trying to rise on the bed.

" Do you feel as though you could walk home?"

" I don't know; I feel kind of faint."

" Does your head pain you?"

" No, sir; it feels numb, and every thing seems to be flying round."

" I dare say."

Harry expressed an earnest desire to go home, and the physician consented to accompany him in a carriage to Mrs. Flint's residence. He had been conveyed in his insensible condition to a house in Boylston Street, the people of which were very kind to him, and used every effort to make him comfortable.

A carriage was procured, and Harry was assisted to enter it; for he was so weak and confused that he could not stand alone. Ben had struck him a terrible blow; and, as the physician declared, it was almost a miracle that he had not been killed.

Mrs. Flint and Katy were shocked and alarmed when they saw the helpless boy borne into the house; but every thing that the circumstances required was done for him.

" Has Edward come home?" he asked, when they had placed him on the bed.

21 *

" No, not yet."

" They will wonder what has beeome of me at the store," eontinued the sufferer, whose thoughts revert-ed to his post of duty.

" I will go down to the store, and tell them what has happened," said Mr. Callender, the kind gentle-man to whose house Harry had been earried, and who had attended him to his home.

" Thank you, sir; you are very good.   I don't want them to think that I have run away, or any thing of that sort."

" They will not think so, I am sure," returned Mr. Callender, as he departed upon his mission.

" Do you think I ean go to the store to-morrow?" asked Harry, turning to the physician.

" I am afraid not; you must keep very quiet for a time."

Harry did not like this announeement.   He had never been sick a day in his life; and it seemed to him just then as though the world could not possibly move on without him to help the thing along.   A great many persons eherish similar notions, and can-not afford to be sick a single day.

I should like to tell my readers at some length what blessings come to us while we are sick ; what angels with healing ministrations for the soul visit the couch of pain ; what holy thoughts are sometimes kindled in the darkened chamber; what noble resolutions have their birth in the heart when the head is pillowed on the bed of sickness. But my remaining space will not permit it; and I content myself with remarking, that sickness in its place is just as great a blessing as health ; that it is part of our needed discipline. When any of my young friends are sick, therefore. let them yield uncomplainingly to their lot, assured that He who hath them in his keeping "doeth all things well."

Harry was obliged to learn this lesson ; and when the pain in his head began to be almost intolerable, he fretted and vexed himself about things at the store. He was not half as patient as he might have been ; and, during the evening, he said a great many hard things about Ben Smart, the author of his misfortune. I am sorry to say he cherished some malignant, revengeful feelings towards him, and looked forward with a great deal of satisfaction to the time when he should be arrested and punished for his crime.

Both Mr. Wake and Mr. Wade called upon him as soon as they heard of his misfortune. They were very indignant when they learned that Harry was suffering for telling the truth. They assured him that they should miss him very much at the store, but they would do the best they could — which, of course, was very pleasant to him. But they told him they could get along without him, bade him not fret, and said his salary should be paid just the same as though he did his work.

"Thank you! thank you! You are very good," exclaimed Harry.

"Yes," Mr. Wake continued; "and, as it will cost you more to be sick, we will raise your wages to four dollars a week. What do you say, Wade?"

"Certainly," replied the junior, warmly.

There was no possible excuse for fretting now. With so many kind friends around him, he had no excuse for fretting; but his human nature rebelled at his lot, and he made himself more miserable than the pain of his wound could possibly have made him

Mrs. Flint, who sat all night by his bed side, labored in vain to make him resigned to his situation. It seemed as though the great trial of his lifetime had come — that which he was least prepared to meet and conquer.

The next day, he was very feverish. His head ached, and the pain of his wound was very severe His moral condition was, if possible, worse than on the preceding night. He was fretful, morose, and unreasonable towards those kind friends who kept vigil around his bed side. Strange as it may seem, and strange as it did seem to himself, his thoughts seldom reverted to the little angel. Once, when he thought of her extended on the bed of pain as he was then, her example seemed to reproach him. She had been meek and patient through all her sufferings — had been content to die, even, if it was the will of the Father in heaven. With a peevish exclamation, he drove her — his guardian angel, as she often seemed to him — from his mind, with the reflection that she could not have been as sick as he was, that she did not endure as much pain as he did For several days he remained in pretty much the same state. His head ached, and the fever burned in his veins. His moral symptoms were not improved, and he continued to snarl and growl at those who took care of him.

"Give me some cold water, marm; I don't want your slops," fretted he, when Mrs. Flint brought him his drink.

"But the doctor says you mustn't have cold water." It was twenty-five years ago.

"Confound the doctor! Give me a glass of cold water, and I will —— "

The door opened then, causing him to suspend the petulant words; for one stood there whose good opinion he valued more than that of any other person.

"O Harry! I am so sorry to see you so sick!" exclaimed Julia Bryant, rushing to his bed side.

She was followed by her father and mother; and Katy had admitted them unannounced to the chamber.

"Julia! is it you?" replied Harry, smiling for the first time since the assault.

"Yes, Harry; I hope you are better. When I heard about it last night, I would not give father any peace till he promised to bring me to Boston."

"Don't be so wild, Julia," interposed her mother.
"You forget that he is very sick."

"Forgive me, Harry; I was so glad and so sorry.
I hope I didn't make your head ache," she added, in
a very gentle tone.

"No, Julia. It was very good of you to come
and see me."

Harry felt a change come over him the moment
she entered the room. The rebellious thoughts in
his bosom seemed to be banished by her presence;
and though his head ached and his flesh burned as
much as ever, he somehow had more courage to endure them.

After Mr. and Mrs. Bryant had asked him a few
questions, and expressed their sympathy in proper
terms, they departed, leaving Julia to remain with
the invalid for a couple of hours.

"I did not expect to see you, Julia," said Harry,
when they had gone.

"Didn't you think I would do as much for you
as you did for me?"

"It was rather different with you. I am only a
poor boy, and you are a rich man's child."

" Pooh, Harry! Our souls are all of a color. You can't think how bad I felt when father got **Mr. Wake's** letter."

" It's a hard case to be knocked down in **that** way, and laid up in the house for a week or two."

' I know it; but we must be patient."

" Can't be patient. I haven't any patience — not a bit. If I could get hold of Ben Smart, I would choke him. I hope they will catch him, and send him to the state prison for life."

Julia looked sad. These malignant words did not sound like those of the Harry West she had known and loved. They were so bitter that they curdled the warm blood in her veins, and the heart of Harry seemed less tender than before.

" Harry," said she, in soft tones, and so sad that he could not but observe the change which had come over her.

" Well, Julia."

" You don't mean what you said."

" Don't mean it? "

" No, I am sure you don't. Do you remember what the Bible says ? "

" What does it say ? " asked he, deeply impressed by the sad and solemn tones of the little angel.

" ' Forgive your enemies,' Harry."

" Forgive Ben Smart, after he has almost killed me ? "

Julia took up the Bible, which lay on the table by the bed side, — it was the one she had given him, — and read several passages upon the topic she had introduced.

Harry was ashamed of himself. The gentle rebuke she administered touched his soul, and he thought how peevish and ill-natured he had been.

" You have been badly hurt, Harry, and you are very sick. Now, let me ask you one question: Which would you rather be, Harry West, sick as you are, or Ben Smart, who struck the blow ? "

" I had rather be myself," replied he, promptly

" You ought to be glad that you are Harry West, instead of Ben Smart. Sick as you are, I am sure you are a great deal happier than he can be, even if he is not punished for striking you."

" You are right, Julia. I have been very wicked Here I have been grumbling and growling all the

22

time for four days. I have learned better. It is
lucky for me that I am Harry, instead of Ben. '

"I am sure I have been a great deal better since
I was sick than before. When I lay on the bed,
hardly able to move, I kept thinking all the time;
and my thoughts did me a great deal of good."

Harry had learned his lesson, and Julia's presence
was indeed an angel's visit. For an hour longer she
sat by his bed, and her words were full of inspira-
tion; and when her father called for her, he could
hardly repress a tear as she bade him good night.

After she had gone Harry begged Mrs. Flint and
Katy to forgive him for being so cross, promising to
be patient in the future. And he kept his promise.
The next day, Julia came again. She read to him,
conversed with him about the scenes of the preceding
autumn in the woods, and told him again about her
own illness. In the afternoon, she bade him a final
adieu, as she was to return that day to her home.

The patience and resignation which he had learned
gave a favorable turn to his sickness, and he began
to improve. It was a month, however, before he was
able to take his place in the store again. Without

the assistance of Julia, perhaps, he had not learned the moral of sickness so well. As it was, he came forth from his chamber with truer and loftier motives, and with a more earnest desire to lead the true life.

Ben Smart had been arrested ; and, shortly after his recovery, Harry was summoned as a witness at his trial. It was a plain case ; and Ben was sent to the house of correction for a long term

CHAPTER XX.

IN WHICH HARRY PASSES THROUGH HIS SEVEREST TRIAL, AND ACHIEVES HIS GREATEST TRIUMPH.

THREE years may appear to be a great while to the little pilgrim through life's vicissitudes; but they soon pass away and are as "a tale that is told." To note all the events of Harry's experience through this period, would require another volume; therefore I can only tell the reader what he was, and what results he had achieved in that time. It was filled with trials and temptations, not all of which were overcome without care and privation. Often he failed, was often disappointed, and often was pained to see how feebly the Spirit warred against the Flesh.

He loved money, and avarice frequently prompted him to do those things which would have wrecked his bright hopes. That vision of the grandeur and influence of the rich man's position sometimes delud-

ed him, causing him to forget for a time that the soul
would live forever, while the body and its treasures
would perish in the grave. As he grew older, he
reasoned more; his principles became more firmly
fixed; and the object of existence assumed a more
definite character. He was an attentive student, and
every year not only made him wiser, but better. I
do not mean to say that Harry was a remarkably
good boy, that his character was perfect, or any
thing of the kind. He meant well, and tried to do
well, and he did not struggle in vain against the trials
and temptations that beset him. I dare say, those
with whom he associated did not consider him much
better than themselves. It is true, he did not swear,
did not frequent the haunts of vice and dissipation,
did not spend his Sundays in riding about the country; yet he had his faults, and captious people did
not fail to see them.

He was still with Wake and Wade, though he was
a salesman now, on a salary of five dollars a week.
He still boarded with Mrs. Flint, though Edward was
no longer his room mate. A year had been sufficient
to disgust his "fast" companion with the homely fare

and homely quarters of his father's house; and, as his salary was now eight dollars a week, he occupied a room in the attic of a first class hotel.

Harry was sixteen years old, and he had three hundred dollars in the Savings Bank. He might have had more, if he had not so carefully watched and guarded against the sin of avarice. He gave some very handsome sums to the various public charities, as well as expended them in relieving distress wherever it presented itself. It is true, it was sometimes very hard work to give of his earnings to relieve the poor; and if he had acted in conformity with the nature he had inherited, he might never have known that it was "more blessed to give than to receive." As he grew older, and the worth of money was more apparent, he was tempted to let the poor and the unfortunate take care of themselves; but the struggle of duty with parsimony rendered his gifts all the more worthy.

Joe Flint had several times violated his solemn resolution to drink no more ardent spirits; but Harry, who was his friend and confidant, encouraged him, when he failed, to try again; and it was now nearly a year since he had been on a "spree."

Our hero occasionally heard from Rockville; and a few months before the event we are about to narrate, ne had spent the pleasantest week of his life with Julia Bryant, amid those scenes which were so full of interest to both of them.   As he walked through the woods where he had first met the " little angel," — she had now grown to be a tall girl, — he could not but recall the events of that meeting.   It was there that he first began to live, in the true sense of the word.   It was there that he had been born into a new sphere of moral existence.

Julia was still his friend, still his guiding star. Though the freedom of childish intimacy had been diminished, the same heart resided in each, and each felt the same interest in the other.   The correspondence between them had been almost wholly suspended, perhaps by the interference of the " powers " at Rockville, and perhaps by the growing sense of the " fitness of things " in the parties.   But they occasionally met, which amply compensated for the deprivations which propriety demanded.

But I must pass on to the closing event of my story — it was Harry's severest trial, yet it resulted in his most signal triumph.

Edward Flint was always short of money. He lived extravagantly, and his increased salary was insufficient to meet his wants. When Harry saw him drive a fast horse through the streets on Sundays, and hear him say how often he went to the theatre, what balls and parties he attended, — when he observed how elegantly he dressed, and that he wore a gold chain, a costly breast pin, and several rings, — he did not wonder that he was " short." He lived like a prince, and it seemed as though eight dollars a week would be but a drop in the bucket in meeting his expenses.

One day, in his extremity, he applied to Harry for the loan of five dollars. Our hero did not like to encourage his extravagance ; but he was good-natured, and could not well avoid doing the favor, especially as Edward wanted the money to pay his board. However, he made it the occasion for a friendly remonstrance, and gave the spendthrift youth some excellent advice. Edward was vexed at the lecture ; but, as he obtained the loan, he did not resent the kindly act.

About a fortnight after, Edward paid him the

money. It consisted of a two dollar bill and six half dollars. Harry was about to make a further application of his views of duty to his friend's case, when Edward impatiently interrupted him, telling aim that, as he had got his money, he need not preach. This was just before Harry went home to dinner.

On his return, Mr. Wake called him into the private office; and when they had entered, he closed and locked the door. Harry regarded this as rather a singular proceeding; but, possessing the entire confidence of his employers, it gave him no uneasiness.

" Harry," Mr. Wake began, " we have been losing money from the store for the last year, or more. I have missed small sums a great many times."

" Indeed ! " exclaimed Harry, not knowing whether he was regarded as a confidant, or as the suspected person.

" To-day I gave a friend of mine several marked coins, with which he purchased some goods. These coins have all been stolen."

" Is it possible, sir ! "

" Now, we have four salesmen besides yourself. Which stole it ? "

"I can form no idea, sir," returned Harry "I can only speak for myself."

"O, well, I had no suspicion that it was you,' added Mr. Wake, with a smile. "I am going to try the same experiment again ; and I want you to keep your eyes on the money drawer all the rest of the afternoon."

"I will do so, sir."

Mr. Wake took several silver coins from his pocket, and scratched them in such a way that they could be readily identified, and then dismissed Harry, with the injunction to be very vigilant.

When he came out of the office, he perceived that Edward and Charles Wallis were in close conversation.

"I say, Harry, what's in the wind?" asked the former, as our hero returned to his position behind the counter.

Harry evaded answering the question, and the other two salesmen, who were very intimate, and whose tastes and amusements were very much alike, continued their conversation. They were evidently aware that something unusual had occurred, or was about to occur.

Soon after, a person appeared at the counter and purchased a dozen spools of cotton, offering two half dollars in payment. Harry kept his eye upon the money drawer, but nothing was discovered. From what he knew of Edward's mode of life, he was prepared to believe that he was the guilty person.

The experiment was tried for three days in succession before any result was obtained. The coins were always found in the drawer; but on the fourth day, when they were very busy, and there was a great deal of money in the drawer, Harry distinctly observed Edward, while making change, take several coins from the till. The act appalled him; he forgot the customer to whose wants he was attending, and hastened to inform Mr. Wake of the discovery.

" Where are you going, Harry? " asked Edward, as he passed him.

" Only to the office," replied he ; and his appearance and manner might have attracted the attention of any skilful rogue.

" Come, Harry, don't leave your place," added Edward, playfully grasping him by the collar, on his return.

" Don't stop to fool, Edward," answered Harry, as he shook him off, and took his place at the counter again.

He was very absent-minded the rest of the fore-noon, and his frame shook with agitation, as he heard Mr. Wake call Edward, shortly after. But he trembled still more when he was summoned also, for it was very unpleasant business.

" Of course, you will not object to letting me see the contents of your pockets, Edward," said Mr. Wake, as Harry entered the office.

" Certainly not, sir ; " and he turned every one of his pockets inside out.

Not one of the decoy pieces was found upon him, or any other coins, for that matter ; he had no money. Mr. Wake was confused, for he fully expected to con-vict the culprit on the spot.

" I suppose I am indebted to this young man for th is," continued Edward, with a sneer. " I'.l bet five dollais he stole the money himself, if any has been stolen. Why don't you search him ? "

" Search me, sir, by all means," added Harry ; and he began to turn his pockets out.

From his vest pocket he took out a little parcel wrapped in a shop bill.

" What's that ? " said Edward.

" I don't know. I wasn't aware that there was any such thing in my pocket."

" I suppose not," sneered Edward.

" But you seem to know more about it than he Edward," remarked Mr. Wake, as he took the parcel.

" I know nothing about it."

The senior opened the wrapper, and to his surprise and sorrow, found it contained two of the marked coins. But he was not disposed hastily to condemn Harry. He could not believe him capable of stealing; besides, there was something in Edward's manner which seemed to indicate that our hero was the victim of a conspiracy.

" As he has been so very generous towards me, Mr. Wake," interposed Edward, " I will suggest a means by which you may satisfy yourself. My mother keeps Harry's money for him; and perhaps, if you look it over, you will find some more marked pieces."

" Mr. Wake, I'm innocent," protested Harry, when he had in some measure recovered from the first shock of the heavy blow. "I never stole a cent from any body."

"I don't believe you ever did, Harry. But can you explain how this money happened to be in your pocket?"

"I cannot, sir. If you wish to look at my money, Mrs. Flint will show it to you."

"Perhaps I had better."

"Don't let him go with you, though," said Edward, maliciously.

Mr. Wake wrote an order to Mrs. Flint, requesting her to exhibit the money, and Harry signed it. The senior then hastened to Avery Street.

"Now, Master Spy!" sneered Edward, when he had gone. "So you have been watching me. I thought as much."

"I only did what Mr. Wake told me to do," replied Harry, exceedingly mortified at the turn the investigation had taken.

"Humph! That is the way with you psalm-singers. Steal yourself, and lay it to me!"

"I did not steal. I never stole in my life.'

"Wait and see.'

In about half an hour Mr. Wake returned.

"I am sorry, Harry, to find that I have been mistaken in you. Is it possible that one who is outwardly so correct in his habits should be a thief? But your career is finished," said he, very sternly, as he entered the office.

"Nothing strange to the rest of us," added Edward. "I never knew one yet who pretended to be so pious, that did not turn out a rascal."

"And such a hypocrite!"

"Mr. Wake, I am neither a thief nor a hypocrite," replied Harry, with spirit.

"I found four of the coins, — four half dollars. — which I marked first, at Mrs. Flint's," said the senior, severely.

Harry was astounded. Those half dollars were part of the money paid him by Edward, and he so explained how they came in his possession.

"Got them from me!" exclaimed Edward, with well-feigned surprise. "I never borrowed a cent of him in my life; and, of course, never paid him a cent."

Harry looked at Edward, amazed at the coolness

with which he uttered the monstrous lie. He q ies-
tioned him in regard to the transaction, but the young
reprobate reiterated his declaration with so much
force and art, that Mr. Wake was effectually de-
ceived.

Our hero, conscious of his innocence, however
strong appearances were against him, behaved with
considerate spirit, which so irritated Mr. Wake that
he sent for a constable, and Harry soon found himself
in Leverett Street Jail. Strange as it may seem to
my young friends, he was not very miserable there.
He was innocent, and he depended upon that special
Providence which had before befriended him, to ex-
tricate him from the difficulty. It is true, he wondered what Julia would say when she heard of his
misfortune. She would weep and grieve ; and he
was sad when he thought of her. But she would be
the more rejoiced, when she learned that he was innocent. The triumph would be in proportion to the
trial.

On the following day he was brought up for examination. As his name was called, the propriety of
the court was suddenly disturbed by an exclamation

of surprise from an elderly man, with a sun-browned face and monstrous whiskers.

" Who is he ? ' almost shouted the elderly man, regardless of the dignity of the court.

An officer was on the point of turning him out : but his earnest manner saved him. Pushing his way forward to Mr. Wake, he questioned him in regard to the youthful prisoner.

" Strange ! I thought he was dead ! " muttered the elderly man, in the most intense excitement.

The examination proceeded. Harry had a friend who had not been idle, as the sequel will show.

Mr. Wake first testified to the facts we have already related; and the lawyer, whom Harry's friends had provided, questioned him in regard to the prisoner's character and antecedents. Edward Flint was then called. He was subjected to a severe cross examination by Harry's counsel, in which he repeatedly denied that he had ever borrowed or paid any money to the accused.

Mr. Wade was the next witness. While the events preceding Harry's arrest were transpiring, he had been absent from the city, but had returned early in

23 *

the afternoon. He disagreed with his partner in relation to our hero's guilt, and immediately set himself to work to unmask the conspiracy, for such he was persuaded it was.

He testified that, a short time before, Edward had requested him to pay him his salary two days before it was due, assigning as a reason the fact that *he owed Harry five dollars* which he wished to pay. He produced two of the marked half dollars, which he had received from Edward's landlady. ˙

Of course, Edward was utterly confounded; and to add to his confusion, he was immediately called to the stand again. This time his coolness was gone; he crossed himself a dozen times, and finally acknowledged, under the pressure of the skilful lawyer's close questioning, that Harry was innocent. He had paid him the money found in Mrs. Flint's possession, and had slipped the coins wrapped in the shop bills into his pocket, when he took him by the collar on his return from the office.

He had known for some time that the partners were on the watch for the thief. He had heard them talking about the matter; but he supposed he had

managed the case so well as to exonerate himself,
and implicate Harry, whom he hated for being a
good boy.

Harry was discharged. His heart swelled with
gratitude for the kindly interposition of Providence.
The trial was past — the triumph had come.

Mr. Wake, Mr. Wade, and other friends, congratulated him on the happy termination of the affair;
and while they were so engaged the elderly man
elbowed his way through the crowd to the place
where Harry stood.

" Young man, what is your father's name?" he
asked, in tones tremulous with emotion.

" I have no father," replied Harry.

" You *had* a father — what was his name?"

" Franklin West; a carpenter by trade. He went
from Redfield to Valparaiso when I was very young,
and we never heard any thing from him.

" My son!" exclaimed the stranger, graspirg our
hero by the hand, while the tears rolled down his
brown visage.

Harry did not know what to make of this announcement.

" Is it possible that you are my father?" asked he

" I am, Harry; but I was sure you were dead. I got a letter, informing me that your mother and the baby had gone; and about a year after, I met a man from Rockville, who told me you had died also."

" It was a mistake."

They continued the conversation as they walked from ne court room to the store. There was a long story for each to tell. Mr. West confessed that, for two years after his arrival at Valparaiso, he had accomplished very little. He drank hard, and brought on a fever, which had nearly carried him off. But that fever was a blessing in disguise; and since his recovery he had been entirely temperate. He had nothing to send to his family, and shame prevented him from even writing to his wife. He received the letter which conveyed the intelligence of the death of his wife and child, and soon after learned that his remaining little one was also gone.

Carpenters were then in great demand in Valparaiso. He was soon in a condition to take contracts, and fortune smiled upon him. He had rendered himself independent, and had now returned to spend his remaining days in his native land. He had been in Boston a week, and happened to stray into the Police Court, where he had found the son who, he supposed, had long ago been laid in the grave.

Edward Flint finished his career of "fashionable dissipation" by being sentenced to the house of correction. Just before he was sent over, he confessed to Mr. Wade that it was he who had stolen Harry's money, three years before.

The next day Harry obtained leave of absence, for the purpose of accompanying his father on a visit to Redfield. He was in exuberant spirits. It seemed as though his cup of joy was full. He could hardly realize that he had a father — a kind, affectionate father — who shared the joy of his heart.

They went to Redfield; but I cannot stop to tel. my readers how astonished Squire Walker, and Mr. Nason, and the paupers were, to see the spruce young clerk come to his early home, attended by his fathe· — a rich father, too.

We can follow our hero no farther through th. highways and byways of his life-pilgrimage. We have seen him struggle like a hero through tria. his

temptation, and come off conqueror in the end.   He
has found a rich father, who crowns his lot with p en
ty ; but his true wealth is in those good princi; es
which the trials, no less than the triumphs, o his
career have planted in his soul.

CHAPTER XXI.

IN WHICH HARRY IS VERY PLEASANTLY SITUATED, AND THE STORY COMES TO AN END.

PERHAPS my young readers will desire to know something of Harry's subsequent life; and we will "drop in" upon him at his pleasant residence in Rockville, without the formality of an introduction. Ten years have elapsed since we parted with him, after his triumphant discharge from arrest. His father did not live long after his return to his native land; and when he was twenty-one, Harry came into possession of a handsome fortune. But even wealth could not tempt him to choose a life of idleness; and he went into partnership with Mr. Wade, the senior retiring at the same time. The firm of Wade and West is quite as respectable as any in the city.

Harry is not a slave to business; and he spends a portion of his time at his beautiful place in Rockville; for the cars pass through the village, which is only a ride of an hour and a half from the city.

Mr. West's house is situated on a gentle eminence not far distant from the turnpike road. It is built upon the very spot where the cabin of the charcoal burners stood, in which Harry, the fugitive, passed two nights The aspect of the place is entirely changed, though the very rock upon which our hero ate the sumptuous repast the little angel brought him may be seen in the centre of the beautiful garden, by the side of the house. Mr. West often seats himself there to think of the events of the past, and to treasure up the pleasant memories connected with the vicinity.

The house is elegant and spacious, though there is nothing gaudy or gay about it. Let us walk in It is plainly furnished, though the articles are rich and tasteful. This is the sitting room. Who is that beautiful lady sitting at the piano-forte? Do you not recognize her, gentle reader? Of course you do. It is Mrs. West, and an old acquaintance. She is no longer the *little* angel, though I cannot tell her height or her weight; but her husband thinks she is just as much an angel now as when she fed him on doughnuts upon the flat rock in the garden.

Ah, here comes Harry! He is a fine-looking man, rather tall; and though he does not wear a mustache, I have no doubt Mrs. West thinks he is handsome — which is all very well, provided he does not think so himself.

"This is a capital day, Julia; suppose we ride over to Redfield, and see friend Nason," said Mr. West.

"I shall be delighted," replied Julia.

The horse is ordered; and as they ride along, the gentleman amuses his wife with the oft-repeated story of his flight from Jacob Wire's.

"Do you see that high rock, Julia?" he asked, pointing over the fence.

"Yes."

"That is the very one where I dodged Leman, and took the back track; and there is where I knocked the bull-dog over."

They arrive at the house of Mr. Nason. It is a pleasant little cottage, for he is no longer in the service of the town. It was built by Mr. West ex

24

pressly for him.   Connected with it is a fine farm of twenty acres.   This little property was sold to Mr Nason by his protégé, though no money was paid. Harry would have made it a free gift, if the pride of his friend would have permitted; but it amounts to the same thing.

Mr. West and his lady are warmly welcomed by Mr. Nason and his family.   The ex-keeper is an old man now.   He is a member of the church, and considered an excellent and useful citizen.   He still calls Mr. West his " boy," and regards him with mingled pride and admiration.

Our friends dine at the cottage; and, after dinner, Mr. Nason and Mr. West talk over old times, ride down to Pine Pleasant, and visit the poorhouse. Great changes have come over Redfield.   Squire Walker, Jacob Wire, and most of the paupers who were the companions of our hero, are dead and gone, and the living speak gently of the departed.

At Pine Pleasant, they fasten the horse to a tree, and cross over to the rock which was Harry's favorite resort in childhood

' By the way, Harry, have you heard any thing of Len Smart lately?" asks Mr. Nason.

"After his discharge from the state prison, I heard that he went to sea."

"He was a bad boy."

"And a bad man."

"I believe he killed his mother. They say she never smiled after she gave him up as a hopeless case."

"Poor woman! I pity a mother whose son turns out badly. What a wreck of fond hopes!"

"Just so," added Mr. Nason.

After visiting various interesting localities, Mr. West and his lady return home. In their absence, a letter for Julia from Katy Flint has arrived. The Flint family are now in good circumstances. Joe is a steady man, and, with Harry's assistance, has purchased an interest in the stable formerly kept by Major Phillips, who has retired on a competency.

"What does she say, Julia?" asked Harry, as she broke the seal.

"They have heard from Edward."

"Bad news, I am afraid. He was a hard boy."

" Yes; he has just been sent to the Maryland penitentiary for house breaking."

" I am sorry for him."

" Katy says her mother feels very badly about it."

" No doubt of it. Mrs. Flint is an excellen woman; she was a mother to me."

" She says they are coming up to Rockville next week."

" Glad of that; they will always be welcome beneath my roof. I must call upon them to-morrow when I go to the city."

" Do; and give my love to them."

And, here, reader, I must leave them — not without regret, I confess, for it is always sad to part with warm and true-hearted friends; but if one must leave them, it is pleasant to know that they are happy, and are surrounded by all the blessings which make life desirable, and filled with that bright hope which reaches beyond the perishable things of this world. It is cheering to know that one's friends, after they have fought a hard battle with foes without and foes within, have won the victory, and are receiving their reward.

If my young friends think well of Harry, let me
admonish them to imitate his virtues, especially his
perseverance in trying to do well; and when they
fail to be as good and true as they wish to be, to
TRY AGAIN.

22 *